Escape

Diamondsong

A Concerto in Ten Parts

Part 01:

Escape

E.D.E. Bell

Atthis Arts
Detroit, Michigan

Diamondsong

Part 01: Escape

Cover Art by M.C. Krauss

Map of Ada-ji by Ulla Thynell

Editorial Services by:
Camille Gooderham Campbell
Catherine Jones Payne and Haley Tomaszewski, Quill Pen Editorial
M. Cusack and G.C. Bell

Published by Atthis Arts, LLC
Detroit, Michigan
atthisarts.com

ISBN 978-1-945009-16-7

Library of Congress Control Number: 2018906188

First Edition: Published June 2018

This book is dedicated to you.

Preface

I hope you're interested in something different.

This series is full of experiments. Most of all, I want readers to like it, so I've taken feedback on the elements people have enjoyed the most from my writing and tried to focus on those strengths.

To me, one of the most striking elements of *Diamondsong* is the code of etiquette that its societies follow. This code includes a lack of assumptions about people—their family makeup, their gender, their attractions—which substantially changes the tone of character introductions. This also institutes gender-neutral pronouns, in addition to a set of gender-spectrum pronouns for those not identifying as primarily masculine or feminine. I urge you to settle in and enjoy these aspects; you will find yourself getting used to them quickly, as the editors and I have. Just writing within the guidelines of Ada-ji has caused me to see our own world in a strikingly new light.

Unexpectedly, the experiment that turned out to be the most challenging was my goal to minimize violence within the story while creating an epic fantasy feel. I included a few elements of violence to contrast concealment versus sheltering, but for the most part the storyline does not rely on violent threats or violent solutions to induce tension or excitement. This was much more difficult than even I expected. I did conclude that how influenced we are by our entertainment is an important subject for continued consideration.

I am proud of the gender distribution I've achieved throughout the storyline, including the type of characters needed, or not needed, to anchor a scene or plotline. As it's even taken me a while to understand what that really means, I hesitate to bias the reader with labels. Statistically, I am thrilled to say that my own readers are equally balanced by gender and not so worried about the endpoints, so I hope each of you will enjoy what I've done.

In all of this love and experimentation, I hope that I've achieved something worthy of your interest. In other words, I worked hard on this and I hope you like it!

I am grateful, as always, to those who helped bring this project to fruition. I couldn't have created this unique series without George Bell. I hope he knows that I know that and knows how much I like him. I am wonderfully grateful for the partnership and friendship of Camille Gooderham Campbell throughout this process. Thanks to Catherine Jones Payne for working this in and for the insightful assessments. My gratitude to Haley Tomaszewski—one of my primary inspirations for this story was a single suggestion she made on *The Scattered Bond*—I hope I did it justice! I'm so appreciative for the generous contributions of G. Mark Cole and Lois Reynolds to the project's funding. And many thanks to the beta readers: Meghan Cusack, Sasha Kasoff Moore, Kimberly Downing, and Trowby Brockman. Thanks to Mom and Mom B for their continued encouragement. To Gwynn, Vance, and Vera—my eternal thanks for supporting this wild ride. That means so much.

And my best gratitude, offered in the truest sense, to each of you who read and enjoy what I do.

E.D.E. Bell
June 2018

THE WORLD OF ADA-JI

The Ja-lal: A humanoid species, dwelling in the foothills and plains of Ada-ji, characterized by broad advancements in construction, invention, and health.

The Fo-ror: A winged humanoid species, dwelling in the forests of Ada-ji, characterized by their rumored use of magical powers, known as valence. The Ja-lal call them fairies.

The Ja-lal and Fo-ror are similar in form, with gray skin, but differences between them in composition and culture. Pyr is singular for a Ja-lal or Fo-ror and pyrsi is plural.

The pyrsi of Ada-ji hold many **gender identities**. While this doesn't clarify all aspects of gender, it is polite to introduce oneself with a prefix, indicating the appropriate pronouns:

- **Fe'** indicates a set of feminine identities, using the pronouns she/her/her(s).
- **Ma'** indicates a set of masculine identities, using the pronouns he/him/his.
- **Ji'** indicates a set of spectrum identities, using the pronouns ve/ver/vis.

When gender is unknown, it is polite to refer to a pyr with xe/xem/xyr(s). Any group of pyrsi (plural) would be referred to with they/them/their(s).

A pyr may be generically referred to as **Burge**, short for the more formal Burgess, often for purposes of polite address or getting a stranger's attention. This is similar to the use of Sir or Ma'am on Earth. For those who hold social prejudice based on class, the term implies some sense of status or honor.

Ja-lal and Fo-ror may live up to 50 cycles. Their lives are divided into defined **epochs**, aligning with societal expectations:

Aoch Age 0-9 Characterized by upbringing, education, and exploration

Bakh Age 10-19 Centered on building family, performing and completing apprenticeships, and finalizing life plans

Gamh Age 20-29 Fully immersed in their specialty or role, contributing full-time to society

Dorh Age 30-39 Respected in leadership and/or advisory roles; it is normal to take some time for self

Eroh Age 40+ Expected to retire and engage in craft or occasional consulting, through the **life expectancy of around 50 cycles**.

Expectations differ for each culture. For example, while a Ja-lal must develop xyr profession into a career, a Fo-ror's profession and rank are set based on xyr social class and other historical and cultural factors.

A cycle on Ada-ji is perhaps up to four times the length of an Earth year. So, our main character, at age 20.5 cycles, has lived more than 80 Earth years but, in relation to her life span, could be considered at the **maturity of her early forties** on Earth.

Each **turn** on Ada-ji, a period of day and then night, is significantly longer than an Earth day. As such, pyrsi do not sleep according to light or dark, but instead based on their own needs, lifestyle, profession, and schedule.

The Ja-lal measure time by the periodic sounding of bells; they refer to the resultant time periods with the same term. The Fo-ror are less rigid about time-keeping and refer to the equivalent time period as a span. Each **bell**, or **span**, consists of more than two Earth hours.

Smaller amounts of time are referred to by both cultures as **takes**, which can be thought of as about ten Earth minutes.

The Ja-lal and Fo-ror live on separate sides of the Great Cliff. They have not interacted since the ***Great War***, an event most noted for being the **end of the Violence** on Ada-ji.

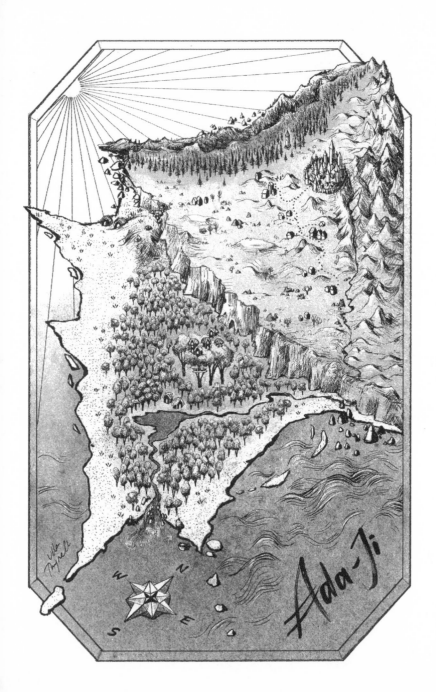

Escape

The first rule is:
Always look the way you're going.

—Dave Ebert, December 1991

Act 1

THE END

Dime had never felt so good.
After cycles of resenting the weight inside her chest and now nearing her middle age—or so she hoped—Dime wasn't going to spend one more turn being bounced around like a miniature in someone else's game.

It had been a long time in her mind, leaving her career, and now she only wondered how she'd delayed so long. Closing the stairwell door behind her, she heaved the wooden crate up onto her living room table. Eager for resolution and then a solid drink, Dime was ready to put what was left of her old life away.

She wasn't sure where to put these last items from her office: a mix of pencils, papers, accessories, and desk baubles. They felt out of place here, at home.

The unexpected irony of closing down her old workspace was that these small possessions stared back at her in duplicate. Her desk drawer cellar of salt; a pair of fingerless gloves for chilly offhours. Another copy of Ma'Rorg's *Quotes for Life*, and a second pair of fidget balls, which chimed as she picked them up.

She wondered if there was a second Dime in there as well.

"I've always wanted a set like yours," Dayn joked from the opposite doorway, the one leading to their cooking and sleeping spaces. Looking down at the gold objects in her hand, she almost tossed them to him, but hesitated, cautious of the delicate outer shells.

With a snort, she threw them anyway, wincing as they landed— not so deftly—into Dayn's outstretched hands. He gave them a couple of turns. "The Intel Circle doesn't know what they've lost," he said in an overly cheerful tone.

They don't care.

He slipped back into their bedroom with a quick but dark grin, the fidget balls still ringing in his fingers—he really was going to take them, wasn't he—and left Dime staring at the stone wall of their tower suite.

Dime appreciated him giving her space today. After cycles of working for the Intel Circle—or IC, as they all called it—first on teams of covert agents and then in strategy and management, she'd finally answered the calling in her heart. The ability to call the game herself, as it were, and not be subject to someone else's dice.

And so, far before her proper time, she'd resigned. Her colleagues, oddly accepting of the idea, had repeated their congratulations over the last several shifts, but for what? What had she done other than leave?

Dayn had supported her decision, of course. He always supported her. As if his career in the Construction Circle weren't as frustrating as her own. He was working an effort literally called the "Boring Project." And Dime was the one who left? Well, it didn't matter now. She'd made up her mind, and she just had to figure it out from here. Relaxing her jaw, she stretched her neck from side to side. *Everything is fine.*

The bells rang through the city and Dime paused to listen to their echoes clanging between Lodon's tall towers. Usually the layered rings of sound reminded her she was running out of time for some project or another. Today, they marked a beginning. A new time. She smiled as the final echoes wafted through a window panel she'd opened for the fresh air. A bird sat on the edge, preening its feathers. Seeing Dime, it flew away.

She enjoyed the light streaming through the open window, warming the room around her. It was a nice home they had found here. On a high floor, for the view, they lived in one of the smaller tower spikes, offshoots of the main tower at its top. There were two suites on this floor, each covering half of the spike, excluding the outer stairwell with its large, vertical windows. While the cooking and bedroom windows faced the other spikes, the living area faced out over the city, its clusters of towers punctuating the view.

She glanced around at the wedge-shaped room as if it were someplace new, rather than familiar. To her left, the broad window curved around the outer wall, clear panels at her height and stained-glass panes across the top, secure within a thick frame of stone. Below it stretched a wide wooden ledge, large enough for sitting and heavily lacquered to protect the burled timber over cycles of use.

A round stand contrasted the wall's sharp corner, holding a potted flowering bush that her older child, Luja, kept vibrant and healthy throughout the seasons. A flat stone wall followed, striped with Dime's tall black bookcases and the door Dayn had disappeared behind. She turned again, to face the wide center fireplace, built into a curved stone wall and feeding into the central chimney.

The final wall, she kept plain, except for a cushioned bench and a few pieces of art, to enjoy the effect of the daylight of Sol, or the nightlight of the skystones, bouncing against its wide stone bricks. The center of the room held their large living table, surrounded by low benches and a couple of mismatched stools. On its edge, sat the crate of items from her office. Her *old* office.

She ran her hand across the smooth boards. Dime had a lot of work to do to figure out how to earn a living now, but at least she could enjoy her own space. Another good reason to get everything put away, she reminded herself.

Reaching into the crate, she squinted at a stack of colorful parchment sleeves. Each was dyed with vibrant natural colors claimed to be from the Undergrowth itself; she'd been saving them for cycles. She picked up the stack and tilted the edges toward her. "Too nice to use," she muttered, sliding them into a drawer at the base of one of the bookshelves.

She set aside a few books and papers, resting them on the window ledge for the moment. Wriggling out a small bundle, she extracted the small roll of fabric into which she'd wrapped her favorite desk ornament. The jade carving was a gift from a Circlemate who'd retired cycles ago; she'd hardly known the pyr. Yet, he'd given her a token purchased from a mountain village: a small jade lizard. He'd said it would bring her wisdom. *That*, she seemed to have disproved.

Unwrapping it, she held the piece in her hand, feeling the cool smoothness of the translucent stone and watching the light from the window dance through to her gray fingers beneath.

Yes, her hands were getting grayer, and not just her hands. Sometimes when Dime glanced in the mirror and saw her darkening face, she realized how much of her life had already passed. *At least now I can live it my way,* she reassured herself, with a twinge of uncertainty she shook aside.

A precise rapping sounded at the door, and she jumped, slipping the jade lizard into a side pouch of her jacket. As old as Dime became, she'd never stop jumping at sudden noises. She pulled the door open.

"So sorry to startle you!" Ador said, a gleam in his eyes.

"You're up to something," Dime said.

"Of course I am," he replied.

Dime smiled with warmth at their friend—one of their oldest and best friends. Though he was closest to her spouse, Dime had long appreciated the elegant pyr with his bright eyes and layered speech patterns.

Their similar height contributed a sliver of his allure, she'd always admitted to herself, but never spoken aloud—even to Dayn. Dime had never understood pyrsi's fascination with height. It wasn't the first societal bar Dime didn't measure up to, nor the last. Still, she could almost look Ador in the eyes, and that was something to enjoy in secret.

As always, he was dressed in finery far in excess of a simple home call. She wasn't sure Ador even owned casual clothes. His tailored mauve pants matched a wide stripe on each side of his long jacket, which was otherwise a dark gray. His cuffs revealed the slightest ruffle, with loops of light lace peeking through. She wondered if the gray fabric was a trick of the eye, meant to make his skin lighter in contrast, giving him a younger appearance. Ador wouldn't care, but the good tailors often employed such tricks. Which was why Dime bought her clothes pre-sewn at the market. Actually.

She ran her gaze across Ador's smiling face. She loved the cohesion of his tattoos; despite his high-class upbringing, he wasn't marked with any symbols of rank or accomplishment. Instead, patterns of abstract waves ran over his scalp and down around his neck. The patterns were unusual, to say the least. He'd lived his life here in rocky Lodon, a city rising tall in all its stone and metal at the base of the mountains, where open water was scarce and transient. As fierce as pyrsi held to the plains and mountains, for one to show symbols of water had a ring of, well, *disloyalty*. At least others might take it that way.

Only two lone symbols stood out; one depicted the Free Winds, an advocacy group Ador led that challenged the Circles' power and structure. The second depicted his announcement as masculine, of ma'pyr, a long time ago now. She had always admired the way he embraced and displayed his own past. Dime tended to avoid her own.

"Here." His hands stretched out to reveal a small yellow box, tied with a sturdy orange string. Taking it, she turned the gift in her hands. "I'm proud of you," he added. Today, of all turns, his gesture touched her, a mix of love and gratitude welling in her chest.

"Oh, Ador. But I haven't done anything."

"What a terrible attitude," he scolded, tapping his fingers against the side of his suit.

"Well," she said, not knowing if she should open the gift in front of him, "I'm not even going anywhere. Besides, I haven't got you a thing." Setting the brightly-colored box on the lacquered window ledge, Dime threw her hands up in a mock gesture.

"What did Sala say?" Ador asked.

It was so like Ador to toss out a casual question about the Light, as if she didn't preside over all of Sol's Reach. The answer wouldn't impress him, though.

"Nothing." Dime had thought, given the work she'd done for the Circles over these many cycles, she might get a visit from the Light. Thanking her or asking why she was leaving. Instead, she'd had a farewell party with a huge tray of bean dip and received a lovely wristband compass. Then she'd taken her crate and left.

"I see. So what happens now?" he asked.

Dime's heart fluttered. Her plan was to start a music school, one that taught a range of life skills. Feeling too self-conscious to talk about it yet, she gave Ador a tailwaggle answer, knowing he'd take it as such.

"Oh, nothing yet. I take a new path, Dayn continues to work his Boring Project"—she heard him grumble from the other room—"and maybe I'll run to the library and pick up a good mystery to settle me for a few turns. Or maybe I'll get out of the city a bit and see Ada-ji. Not just from the depths of some IC den, no—but out, exploring new things."

Her mind did race a bit at the idea of getting out of the city. Make no mistake, she loved Lodon with all her heart. She was born here and had never left for long. She loved Lodon's stone towers, its hills, its ominous crags. She loved the chiseled ravines and the feel of their smooth stones against her bare feet. She loved the warmth of Sol from the top of the Circles' complex, its golden accents shining in the light.

Subconsciously, her hand reached up and felt the crystal which had hung around her neck as long as she could remember. Her father had never said much about it; when she'd asked him, he'd simply said the pendant was hers. Once—and once only—he remarked that he'd named her Diamond for the one around her neck when he'd found her.

But ba'pyrsi weren't born with diamonds. In fact, she'd never seen one other than her own. They were often mentioned in fantasy tales or used as metaphors. Dime would have considered them a myth had she not owned this one. Too visually striking to be any other type of glass or stone, and with a unique octagonal shape, she felt certain it was real.

Dime kept the pendant tucked under her clothing when outside her home. But here, with Sol's rays streaming through the wide window, she liked the way its soft facets caught the light, casting jagged rainbows onto the rough walls.

It always amazed her how something so simple could pull her from the expansive landscape and rising towers of Lodon that spread across the tall tower view of her living space. She released the necklace.

Only at this point did she realize she was gazing wistfully out of her living room window as her friend stood waiting, his hands clasped in patience.

A cool wind swept through the open panel.

Dime threw her hand over a stack of flapping papers, old work logs she had saved but not revisited. "I don't need these now." She shoved the stack into the refuse bin and turned sharp on her toes. "I didn't give up."

His face drawing slightly, Ador waited for her to continue. But Dime understood the truth behind everyone's cautious congratulations. For a pyr well into her Gamh, the epoch of making changes was over. She was supposed to have her plans together far before now. She was supposed to know her path. But, she didn't. It was why she left.

"Actually, I did," she amended. "But it wasn't because I didn't want to try anymore, it was that I didn't think I could make a difference." She paused. With Ador's connections to high-status pyrsi throughout the Circles, he must have known that despite her controversial positions and points of advocacy, she was under Sala's consideration for Intel Chief: a member of the Light's Circle itself.

Yet, having ideas dismissed by a boss still had the same effect no matter which step that boss was on. And—

"Joining the Free Winds ended my own career in the Circles." Ador interrupted her thoughts, his smooth words grating like scratched glass. "I understand more than you think. Sala views it as treason, what we do. Treason! Suggesting pyrsi think for their own harmed selves!" Ador slammed his jaw shut, folding his arms and turning to gaze out of the tower window, where colorful festival banners rippled in the wind.

Ador had been the leader of the Free Winds for so long, Dime was embarrassed to realize she'd never thought of him having a career before that. And one in the Circles, too.

It was so much more than a career that he'd given up; he'd accepted a life of being viewed as high-class, but not accomplished. Intelligent, but not important. She saw him in new light: not just as their kind and insightful friend, but someone braver—more revolutionary—than she had considered.

What else had she missed all these cycles?

Dayn wandered back into the room at a casual pace, as if Ador's harsh language and terse tone had not drawn him in. Dime almost laughed. When Ador started swearing, something was about to get serious.

"I'd best be on my way." Ador smiled with kindness, but his eyes were now distracted.

Dime knew better than to press her friend once he was worked up. She'd call on him later for a glass of ferm and to thank him for the gift. Ador fanned his fingers and, with a nod to Dayn, stepped through the door. It closed behind him with a *thud*.

Her spouse stood across the room, his familiar shape casting a larger shadow against the broad stones of the inside wall. The top of his head—also grayer than she had remembered—sent off a gleam in the bright light. She loved his simplicity, his unassuming stance, his plain suits.

Unlike Ador with his patterns of waves, Dayn was the least

tattooed adult she'd ever seen. And he had no concern what anyone thought of it. Just a few simple images marked him, most prominently a small tattoo for each of their two children, one spectrum and one feminine. Their names rested on Dayn's temples in slanted letters: *Luja. Tum.*

Luja had come to them first, when ve lost vis original parents in a toothcar accident at only two cycles of age. A friend at the medical enclave who knew Dime's own story had said none of the ch'pyr's extended family were able and asked if they'd be interested in parenting. One look at the toddling youth with the sharp expression and they knew their life had changed forever.

Just half a cycle later, a pyr traveled to the city, close to labor and seeking a family for the infant. Without much time to coordinate, the same friend had asked if Dime and Dayn were interested in a second. They'd rushed to the enclave for the birth and fallen instantly in love with the quiet little bundle, tiny eyes searching to meet theirs. A rare condition had impeded the development of Tum's legs, and turns later, they'd been mostly removed. Soon after, they sat around their cozy tower suite as a chaotic little quartet, Dime marveling at her fortune.

She had never become pregnant over the cycles, and not through lack of opportunity, but her family was perfect as-is. Two felt just right. Especially with Dayn spoiling the shoulder pads off both of them. Speaking of which, one of Dayn's shoulder buttons had worked loose.

"Oh, come here," she said to Dayn. "Your button is almost hanging off. We need to—"

As she took a step toward him, she heard a click from behind her. Dayn froze. Spinning around, Dime jumped with a loud gasp as the entry door swung open, revealing three robed figures. Dime screamed, and her limbs locked in place.

They stood like statues, backlit by the stairway window, with dark hoods pulled over their faces, which were obscured in the shadows beneath. They were hunched over, perhaps, or their cloaks rose with exaggerated padding. She didn't have time to understand, as one of the cloaked pyrsi pressed toward her with a span of glittering rope.

"You are under arrest," xe said in a strange, smooth accent, not to the two of them, but directly to Dime, as though they had located someone of great import. "You will come with us to further resolve this matter."

The mysterious pyr moved closer with calm steps, reaching the rope forward.

Who is this? *A rest?* Her thoughts confused, she stumbled in disorientation, coughing at a strong perfume. Why would someone enter her home? Why would they risk wearing hoods, against security statute? Who were—

The figure clasped her arm and started to pull her close. Then xe paused as if stunned, xyr eyes resting on Dime's pendant. She grunted, wrenching her hand away.

By instinct, Dime spun to the side, avoiding xyr next grasp. The figure tripped forward, losing xyr balance. A second figure pushed toward her, almost knocking over Ador's gift, sitting on the ledge. "Don't touch that," Dime snapped, whisking the small box into a jacket pouch without taking her eyes from the dark hood.

My children. An inner voice cut through her panic. Her children. Tum was at lessons and Luja was at apprenticeship. Tum had taken Agni to lessons; she remembered seeing the kita's furry paw curled over Tum's wrap when they'd placed Tum in the bucketpull to be lowered downstairs. That left Dayn, still behind her. They needed to get away. Whatever was happening, Dime only understood she could not let them tie her with any rope.

Out, then. Out.

"Together," she called. As the figures closed in again, Dayn's familiar presence joined her as they grasped hands and bolted from the room like a construction rod. Their pursuers seemed confused by the action, but not for long. As Dime and Dayn tumbled out into the center staircase, Dime's training took over.

If you are detected, get away. Leave no evidence. Get away. Assess and plan later.

Their spike had one primary staircase, centered with a bucket-pull. The first hub was three floors down—one of Dime's favorite spots, where Marn kept fresh brew and always ensured a current copy of the *Caller*. As they barreled toward it, almost flying downward with their hands on the spiral banister, Dime considered what they should do next.

The pyr in their room had put xyr hand on Dime without permission. She couldn't shake the touch of it. Was this what the—the *Violence* felt like? And the ropes. Why? No pyr would consider forcibly detaining another; those who violated the rules accepted being marked by warning hemsa tattoos and left to live out of the city.

Was it possible these pyrsi were from one of the outlaw villages on the edges of Sol's Reach? Had they abandoned all order? With hoods, she couldn't see their hemsa, if they had any. Wearing hoods would earn them more hemsa, if identified, so they must be serious. She had no clue what she was dealing with. Or why. Could they even mean . . . harm?

While Dime saw no other way out than through the hub—for as sure as Sol she wasn't going to submit to these cloaked strangers—she didn't want to put others in their path. Yet they trailed close behind her in the narrow staircase and, the image of their tightly grasped rope muddling her thoughts, she let her feet continue to run.

Dime landed hard in the center of her local hub, glad she was still wearing her boots as they slammed into the planked floor, surrounded by lounging residents and the smell of fresh brew beans. Several pyrsi screamed, scrambling out of her and Dayn's way. "Danger!" Dime shouted. "Danger; leave or hide!"

The hooded figures landed beside them without a stride to spare. One reached for her, getting hold of both arms this time. Involuntarily, Dime yelped. Dayn thrust the wheeled brew stand, brew and all, between them, forcing the aggressor to jump back and release her, as pyrsi in the hub gasped and screamed.

"Go!" Dayn yelled.

Dime jumped onto the counter, kicking the papers as she slid across it. Pages from the *Caller* fluttered into the air and Dime leapt over the side, aiming toward one of the two closest exits, knowing they wouldn't see which one she had chosen until she was through it. She raced forward with all her force, again propelling herself, hand over hand, down each floor's banister.

Purchasing a high home for a nice view now seemed like another of her more short-sighted decisions. Her heart pounding, she tried to remember where each hub was, as now she was in a less familiar section of the tower. The shouts from behind indicated a close pursuit, as did Dayn's voice, carrying over the din. "Go! Go!" he continued to shout.

She realized in that moment what Dayn must already have realized. They wanted *her*. Not Dayn. *Dime.* She was the one that needed to get away.

Unsure how she was able to keep pushing forward, and not feeling much of anything at this point, she continued the pattern: down the tower, find a hub, pick a new, less expected path. Stay one step ahead. Switching spires cost her time, but she hoped it might throw off her pursuers. She only needed to get far enough ahead that they would choose the wrong arch; maybe even enter a new tower once they got to the lower levels.

If she lost them, would they leave?

But she didn't lose them, and she heard a torrent of steps close behind. *What do you want with me?* Dime asked again and again. There must be better options than simply running, but there was no time to think. Floors flashed by, and pyrsi gaped and ran, and Dime gave up on reality until she had time to consider it again. Almost rolling out into the tower's street-floor lobby, she bolted for the entrance.

As though her senses caught up to her, she felt an overwhelming exhaustion all at once. Should she try and find Enforcement? Would these outlaws even respond? Wearing hoods and wielding ropes, they showed complete disregard for the law.

Yet she couldn't keep running this way, with her pursuers right behind her. She could run to a public place, but if the invaders tried to take her anyway, would pyrsi stop them? How could they be stopped if they did not respond to the law? The answers were not ones she would consider.

She thought that in a crowd, she could lose them. They seemed to want her specifically; she hoped they wouldn't use the ropes on anyone else.

Stumbling from the lobby arches as those within fled in panic, she heard the commotion growing behind her. There was a dome just down the street; with a sharp breath, she turned toward it. Pedestrians and toothcars paced by on the busy road. She hoped in desperation that they would block her from view and the pursuers would leave, their mission a failure. Behind her, the calls grew closer. They were gaining ground, almost to her.

She heard a bellowing yell. Turning by instinct, she saw that Dayn had leapt onto the tail end of the closest one's cloak and dug a set of metal claws—Construction Circle pyrsi always carried little tools—into the thick fabric to hook the figure's garments and hold him back so Dime had a better chance of leaving. *No!* It was too close to the Violence. The fabric must have been damaged. She would not allow it.

The figure wrestled away, not understanding that Dayn's tool had burrowed into the cloak, holding it back as xe continued to press forward. As the dark fabric rippled away, two large, iridescent wings sprung back and a rope of braided hair unraveled between them, as if xe hadn't shaved, well, for cycles.

Wings.

Hair.

For a long stride that was probably just a split moment, they froze, staring at each other. The pyr—she supposed xe was still a pyr; xe didn't look so different overall—wore a dark robe, accented with a small pin. Xyr face, what was visible outside of the hair, was much like anyone else's, but without any tattoos.

"Take that one too!" one of the cloaked figures yelled to the uncloaked pyr as xe pointed at Dayn, still in his slippers. "Meet back at Chambers!" Around them, chaos bounced through the crowd like lightning.

"Fairies!" pyrsi shouted, those whose shouts were discernable over the torrent of screams.

"Sprites!"

"Their wings, like bugs!"

"Look! Over there, look!"

"The Violence! The fairies have returned it!"

Dime and Dayn locked eyes. "Don't worry about me," they both called, as if in chorus. Dime wanted to smile, but then it seemed she had two pursuers now to flee, whereas Dayn would just have the one. She'd better get to it.

Fairies?

A knot grew in her gut and her back twitched in a panic spasm as she accepted what she had seen. Whispered stories of the flying creatures flashed through her mind, of their terrifying screams and cruel practices, living in murky forests with the beast-like newts. Yet, there xe was. Clearly a fairy, yet looking like other pyrsi at xyr core, wings and hair aside.

Contact with the fairies would return the Violence. Dime couldn't think about that now, not if she wanted to prevent it.

Around her, pyrsi screamed and ran. Someone pulled the storm siren, and wind rushed through the bellows, its loud warning howling down the street.

The uncloaked fairy with the braided hair flew overhead, pushing aside the abandoned toothcar Dayn had slipped behind as if by valence. But—it must be valence, Dime realized with shock. Then, valence was real?

For all the childhood stories she'd been told about the wicked fairies and the powerful valence of their huge wings, this wasn't quite the power she had imagined. The car rocked and then steadied, but Dayn had already moved far down the street. The fairy, still in flight, grunted and then darted his way.

Two more to evade. Instead of running as Dayn had, Dime jumped behind a row of food carts and made her way to a water ravine, just deeper than her own height. Unsure if her pursuers had seen her lower into it, she darted along the dry streambed, hoping to gain some distance before they figured out where she had gone.

The large, round stones turned under her feet and the dry air burned in her lungs. In addition to her lack of speed, she worried about tripping or turning an ankle. Several turns later, and angry for not having her climbing gloves though there was no reason she would have had them on, Dime's fingers scraped and bled as she pulled herself out of the ravine and into a narrow alley.

Cursing that she could not see the shadows here, she ran again, hoping she was headed toward the city gates. Seeing the still-hooded figures—she supposed these were fairies too—at the end of the alleyway, she turned back and pushed through a crowded shop, racks of ready-made suits smacking her from both sides. She resisted the urge to hide, knowing they had seen her enter. Even risking a hemsa to take clothing for a disguise would not help.

Popping through the shop's main arch, she noted that the rumors had not yet reached this street, as pyrsi glanced up curiously at what must be the false sound of a storm siren. Turning a corner and hoping the fairies wouldn't arrive and see her, Dime hailed a flagged toothcar, trying to catch her breath. "Great Gates, please," she said in her best management voice. "I'm late meeting someone, so if you could hurry."

With a nod, the driver began to pedal, and the toothed wheels gripped and clanked their way down toward the low end of the city. She knew she couldn't rest, but she wasn't sure her legs could have taken another step.

Breathing deeply, she tried to calm the flickering spasms in her back and remember what had happened. She'd just arrived home and started to unpack. Ador had stopped by. And then, three strangers had come in without permission—one had touched her without permission—and then they had all proceeded to disrupt a great many tower floors. It didn't feel real.

Memories flashed by of the glittering rope, the grasp on her wrist, the burn of the old wood against her hands as she jumped and slid from floor to floor of the tower. Her feelings of survival, her singular focus of getting away.

She had escaped the tower to realize her pursuers were not ordinary pyrsi, but the fairies of lore, the fairies from the Undergrowth, far to the sur and over the Great Cliff. Looking not as monsters, but extraordinary pyrsi. Looking *real.*

One of these fairies had flown in pursuit of Dayn, the poor ma'pyr still in his slippers. Two were chasing her now, and perhaps knew she had taken this car. She wasn't sure.

Her heart thumped with worry, and she tried to calm it. She trusted Dayn; he was clever and persistent. He wouldn't let himself be controlled. Besides, they had treated him like a witness. It was Dime they wanted.

But why?

No answers coming to mind, Dime filed through her options. If she had put enough space between them, she could pay the driver and sneak away, to somewhere in the low city. They couldn't search all of Lodon for her. Pyrsi feared and despised the unseen fairies; that was kneaded into them from the moment of birth. But how could the winged beings be stopped?

If she could just get away and hide, then she could *plan.* Paying the driver with an extra rate, she asked to be let out at a nondescript juncture of cafés and shops.

As the car pulled away, pyrsi screamed and scattered. *Harm it!* Turning, she saw the flying figures racing toward her again.

They were flying now as well, without cloaks to conceal their nature. These also had hair: long volumes of hair, shaped as though sculptures of art rather than manes, as they'd always been described. They must have followed her car the whole way, while she was hoping she'd escaped them. Or perhaps they had surveilled the streets below, assuming this was the way she'd go. Either way, they'd found her. *Harm it all, they were good. And stubborn!*

"Submit to your arrest!" a low voice called, as a fairy swooped down toward her. Wallside compost bins, twice the height of a pyrsi, swerved into the street, as if to block her way forward. As in, they moved *on their own*. More valence. Dime shivered.

One of the bins landed unsteadily and toppled over, knocking over a second, which crashed into the building beside it. The wall cracked, releasing a cloud of dust and smoke, and sending bricks down into the street, where many split or crumbled. The fairy darted back and Dime caught a glimpse of xyr eyes; they were frightened.

The smooth voice shook now, against tilted vowels, and Dime could see only the rope that the fairy waved, its strange glitter pronounced through the settling dust and the rising smell of spilled compost. "You must trust me!"

These tactics were dangerous, putting pyrsi in real danger, whether intended or not. She had no idea what values these fairies held or what they might do with their valence if pressed.

She couldn't risk finding out. She had to get out of Lodon. Away from pyrsi, away from her family. If she could get out, she could find a place to hide. She'd send them a message that she was no longer in Lodon. She could keep the intruders away.

Ignoring her shaking legs, she crawled over a heap of rubble and faltered, rolling down into the dusty street before finally regaining her stance. Above her, the fairy let out a loud whistling sound, which she took to be calling the others. At least, then, Dayn was likely safe. For now.

Either way, there were only so many tricks she could employ here, with three flying creatures determined to tie their glittery ropes to her arms for a purpose she could not conceive, knocking down bins in their careless haste. *Out.* She needed to get out.

Walled and nestled into the mountainous crags as Lodon was, the city only had a few reasonable points of entry. Or in her case, exit. Yet, to these flying beings, maybe Lodon's tall walls and rocky dropoffs meant little.

That's it.

If they would continue to pursue her by air, she would use their advantage to her own. She thought about running toward the Arcade; it wasn't far. But she wasn't willing to risk endangering the heavy crowds inside. It was hard to accept this threat of danger, but she had seen the fairy use valence. She had seen the bins move, the bricks flying.

"Ugh." She stopped a moment, catching what remained of her breath and shaking a fist into the air, toward the fairy. "Hey, there!" Dime called. Xe dove toward her, and Dime noted what seemed to be a look of relief. *Don't make assumptions, now.*

Dime darted away, running into an alley. With a final grumble, she heaved open a street vent and slid down toward whatever awaited.

What doesn't kill you— What a silly sentiment. She just hoped it wouldn't kill her. There were pyr-size pipes under the central city, as her father, a long-time worker in the Maintenance Circle, had told her. They ran from the mountains to catch melting snow or strong storms. Some fed the wells and others carried less desirable byproducts out to the massive gulch to the eas. She tried not to think about how far downcity she now was.

And it was the second type of tunnel. Dime couldn't ignore the smell, though she tried to put it from her mind.

Da-da had been right: the tunnels were pyr-sized. Though not so much with this one. Crouching, she shuffled through the murky pipe, glad it was the dry season, yet trying not to imagine what her boots might be imbued with by the time she got out. Sliding her sleeve over her wristband with its little compass, she cursed. It was too dark to see the thin needle, of course. She'd have to figure out which way to go without it.

The light dimmed to nothing as Dime left the open port behind her. She concentrated on each turn, at first imagining where in the city she might be, and then just letting the downward slope guide her.

After a few dozen times bumping her arms against the rough stonemix—how glad she was to have her work jacket on, though it must be torn now—she knew there was no way the winged pyrsi could keep pace with their heavy builds and large wings. Dime was a small pyr and she could barely fit through. Pace after pace, she shuffled through the endless tunnels, dotted only by periodic faint beams of light above.

"Harm's way," she cursed, as she lost her balance at a sharp decline and a hint of Sol's light wafted up the tunnel from its downward slope ahead. She started to slip, her boots sliding down the wet stone. As she fell back into a murky puddle by the ledge that smelled worse than if a public toilet had fallen into a public toilet and then died, she swore again before lifting herself to her feet. Dizzy at the steep incline before her, she carefully turned around, retracing her steps through the darkness until she saw a trace of light ahead.

She hadn't really thought this last part through, but surely Maintenance didn't always rely on their ladders? Ladders could break, they could— Exhaling acidic air from her aching lungs, she ran her hands along the wall. Her fingers stuck into a wide crevice in the stonemix, and she found another above it. Rung by rung she pulled herself up to the top, just to find she could not open the heavy metal grate.

"Hello!" she called. "Hello; a bit of trouble here?" *So this is not me at my most covert.* "Hello?"

She paused, wondering how else she could get attention. She'd always been warned away from the low city, especially its outer rings, for the outlaws and wanderers said to live this close to the gulch. Hopefully there was one around. Her tired fingers started to shake, and it was like meeting the light of Sol verself as the grate groaned and screeched its way over, helped by someone on the other side.

Dime was surprised at the silence from above. She expected by now the whole city would be lit up with the network of storm sirens, warning pyrsi of danger.

A narrow face peered down at her, moving back as Dime climbed through the opening, squinting at the light as she stood to face the pyr. "Ma'Kile," he offered, extending both arms in front. She tried not to look at his hemsa, the tattoo across his forehead marking him as convicted of possessing tzetz. She despised the hemsa; stopping the practice had been her cause. She wanted to reach up to the large mark and touch it, as if her fingers held erasers. But that wasn't how it worked.

He made no note of her smell, or at least didn't show that he had. She reached her own arms out graciously, linking with his to form the bridge. "Fe—" Dime started to introduce herself back, then hesitated. "Hello, Kile," she offered. "It would be best if you didn't mention this. Er, bad day. You know."

Embarrassed at her silly remarks but so tired she could barely even think and wanting to protect him from association with her, she pulled an unsigned paynote from a pouch, and handed it to him. She needed to go. "Thank you. Perhaps you can use that. For . . . my gratitude."

Leaving Kile behind and blinking as her eyes adjusted to the light, she saw the high walls of the low city towering above her. As grand as she had felt in her lofty home with these huge walls little outlines below, she felt quite small at their base. Yet, urgency pumped in her veins, and she wouldn't feel safe until she had reached a den. Hopefully one with a shower.

Hugging the walls of the city, she moved slowly toward the spires of the Great Gates ahead. It was an obvious point of departure; a fairy could be waiting for her there. Yet, she wasn't familiar enough with the side gates to risk not finding one in her current state. Truly, she felt as though she had about two blinks before falling asleep where she stood. The bells rang again, more distant sounding from here; she had been on the run now for a full bell. She didn't think it could be two.

This helped her next decision. Edging toward the main road, she got as close to the line of toothcars as she could. Noting a wide car pedaled by at least eight hired drivers—the type a high-class retiree would take to picnic outside of the city for claims of enjoying nature but mostly to show that xe could—she took her chance.

Rolling from behind a parked toothcar to the side, she dove between the turning wheels. She flipped flat on her back and reached up to grasp the cold, metal frame, pushing her feet against a beam. The car heaved her up and down as it moved; she grew certain it would crush her into the gravel of the street. She heard voices from above, and hoped they weren't inquiring about the smell.

She closed her eyes, trying to stay her nausea. Her fingers grew numb as she forced herself to hold her grip against the metal. Lulled into a trance, she felt the road slope beneath her as it angled downward toward the gates. The car stopped; above her, the drivers answered questions and paid their tolls. *Come on,* she urged. The car lurched forward again, filling her ears with the grating rhythm of its massive, spike-like teeth.

Worried that she couldn't hold on for another stride, she flung herself out from underneath the vehicle, ignoring the shouts and calls of the lounging passengers as she bumped down a slow, scrub-covered hill. Hiding under the low branches of a wide bush, she watched the car stop, then pull away again. A sudden awareness of her exhaustion and thirst hit her, more than any relief of finally being alone. She needed to move on, find a source of water. Get to a den and recover.

She scanned the skies. Dots in the distance hovered near the gates, and her heart dropped knowing she had come all this way and they were still in sight, looking for her. But—perhaps they hadn't seen her. They must not have seen her, or they would be here now, surrounding her.

Dime felt exposed among the dried-out branches; nightfall was still many bells away. She wasn't going to sit in the bush and wither from thirst and be found anyway. Best to go. Keep moving. Until she was certain she could rest.

She sat up, her head spinning. Having spent twenty-plus

cycles never seeing a fairy, it should have been inconceivable that she was watching pyrsi fly like birds and was being chased by a—flock?—of them. And yet the main things on her mind were safety, water, and sleep.

Third-tier schooling had felt a bit this way. One push, following another, following another, and all the time just wanting to rest. Yet just as she had graduated with the recommendation that had got a low-class pyr such as herself in the door at the Circles, she wasn't about to give up now. Her stubborn side was kicking in, as it tended to do when things went wrong. And the fairies didn't see her. She'd be fine.

Dime had no map of the IC's hidden dens with her, and she'd been stuck in the towers for quite a while now. She thought there was one this way, but still at a distance. She couldn't run another step. She couldn't even walk there, not without water or rest.

Looking over at the road, she sighed. *They don't see me.*

She kept her body low, crawling back up the hill toward a small tunnel that cut through a rise in the rocks. Out in the plains or hills, the road would just wind over it, but this close to the city, pyrsi insisted on flat, straight roads. She waited until she saw a tiny toothcar, the sort for day rentals and lavished children, drive into the tunnel. The car looked old and didn't bear a rental flag. Slipping into the tunnel, she popped into the driver's view.

"Excuse me, Burge," she said, as he cranked to a stop. "I have an emergency and need a car to leave the city." She almost flashed her Circles card—they'd forgotten to ask for it back—but she'd always disliked pyrsi using their position for their own gain, and even now, her well-being on the line, she couldn't do it.

Inside, the driver scrunched xyr face, and Dime remembered that she stunk. "Here. For borrowing the car." She pulled out her last unsigned note, a large denomination she kept for emergencies. "Please," she added. "I can't say why, but it's important."

The driver seemed at a loss for words, but after glancing at Dime's forehead then registering the amount of the note, xe stepped out of the car. "If you give me your name," Dime said, "I'll pay you the rest when I return."

"It's enough," xe stammered, waving her away. "Go with Sol."

Dime didn't wait to say more, hopping in and pedaling as carefully as she could, through the tunnel and away from the city. At first she stayed on the road, as there was a moderate size town this way, with frequent travel to and from the city. At a side road that she hoped wouldn't draw attention, she veered off, trying to keep a steady pace and blend in.

Her tired legs ached against the stiff action of the small car, but Dime couldn't afford to stop. Her legs slowed anyway, finally resting on the pedals as her head slumped forward and the car jerked to a halt. There was no way she could continue. Pulses of exhaustion shot down each limb like an exaggerated heartbeat.

No. She couldn't stop here, in the middle of nowhere. She needed to hide. Her family needed her. She needed them. She pictured the fairy's face as xe'd waved the glittering rope. A stabbing pain jolted through her and she began to push the pedals again. Foot after foot, she moved forward. Confused but grateful, she continued on.

The toothcar had flimsy sheetwood panels rather than full doors, but they shielded her from view. Hopefully there were plenty of toothcars dotting the little roads of the plains, so the fairies could not know which to pursue.

Unwilling to show herself by peering out for signs of them in the sky, she pedaled on, barely feeling the pedaling anymore as she focused solely on getting far away.

She stayed on the roads until she was well out in the plains, where the roads were barely paths anyway. Only then did she turn off onto the open plain, trusting the relative steadiness of the rocky terrain, veined with gullies and dotted with lone clusters of dry trees. So dry, so flat, and so vast compared to Lodon. Yet, it was quiet. Free.

Unsure how she was able to continue, Dime pushed on, her thoughts lulling her into some state of calm. She kept an eye on her wristband, letting the little needle, which always pointed sur, guide her to where she thought the closest den was hidden.

Dime had never been fully comfortable with the dens where agents stayed while gathering Intel on the outlying villages; maybe it's why she'd allowed them to move her back into the towers over the cycles. Problem was, she disliked her increasingly administrative tasks even more than the intrusive field work discomfited her—no, she didn't work for the Circles anymore. The thought shocked her, as if it hadn't been her idea in the first place.

Sala had long preached that, to keep pyrsi prosperous and healthy, it was necessary to know what problems as well as resources existed throughout Sol's Reach, even in these small villages that didn't respond so graciously to what they saw as interference from the Circles. Sala saw it as proper Intelligence. Deterrence of crime. Knowledge of assets. Keeping order among pyrsi. In case. Always— in case.

Now Dime worried that she'd passed the hidden den, not having seen the specific stack of rocks indicating an entrance. Not willing to double back, she remembered another in this direction, but it was much farther away.

This den, where Dime had spent one awful rotation, was far out in the plains, and few pyrsi lived out here, away from the mountains and the comforts of the city. The towns were small and their inhabitants suspicious of strangers. She could see why; just the thought of being so close to the fairies sent shivers through her. Literal shivers, as that twitching in her back hadn't quite subsided.

What could fairies want with her? *Fairies!* She couldn't believe she was even thinking it. She'd gone all these cycles doubting whether they were even real—whether there was truly life beyond the Great Cliff—and now here she was, pedaling away across the plains toward the end of Sol's Reach. Frustrated, she accelerated, no longer even affected by the effort of her feet against the pedals.

Dime couldn't imagine what she had done. Sure, there was the hiring incident with Hara's nephew—and what a grudge Hara held over that—and there was Dime's anti-hemsa work, but mostly that just raised discomfort and lost her a few social allies. The peckbeak campaign? No. She propelled the car forward.

She remembered that unbelievable flying pyr silhouetted in Sol's light. The large translucent wings bending the light like the valence they created.

Bottom line: Ok, she now believed in fairies. But what would *fairies* care about any of the minutia of Dime's aging and now inconsequential life?

These thoughts circled as Dime pedaled in the tiny car, bell after bell, though she couldn't hear any actual bells from here. Feeling naked on the vast plains, far from any roads, she hoped the fairies had not followed this far. Surely they'd need to rest; Dime couldn't believe she still hadn't, but necessity drove her onward.

She hoped the toothcar had decent spikes, as the ground was rocky. Even as the car kept moving, Dime's eyes drooped and her arms slumped. As the time passed, her mind went blank.

It truly felt like a dream at this point. She wasn't sure how long she had pedaled anymore, but it felt like forever. Perhaps it was. Perhaps she had never pedaled at all, and any moment she would wake in her bed at home, and Dayn would say oh my how you pedal in your sleep.

That sounded absurd. And Dayn, had he gotten away? She would regroup and she would sleep and then she could find him. She thought of him again, as, to her surprise, one of the Construction Circle's boring sites came into view: tall painted machines pumping sharp blades down into the rock.

They shouldn't be mining down here, in the plains. There was no reason for it. Perhaps that's why Dayn had been so agitated when she brought it up. They were mining in the mountains, where there was endless rock, not down here. She brushed away the first thought that jumped to mind. She wasn't allowed to repeat the rumors. No one was.

Except no one was here to listen. Ok. The diamond mines.

Agents sometimes brought back rumors that diamond mines separated the Undergrowth, the land of the fairies, from her own pyrsi in Sol's Reach. The Chief laughed it off and reminded the team to stick to facts. The Great Cliff separated them, not caves. Except they never talked about fairies. But she had seen fairies, in Lodon. This didn't make sense now. She was feeling so tired.

And Sol's light, but she wasn't going to pee in the car. No matter what stink she was covered in, there were still limits. She pulled the car's brake. Ducking out, she squatted over the parched plains, wondering how far in any direction she could be seen. Whatever. At least she wasn't tied by those glittering ropes, whatever they were. Flinching at the sparkle of her own pendant, she shoved it back into her shirt.

Groggy, she remembered the fairies. She scanned the skies and saw nothing but clouds. She had made it away, or so it seemed. Then all she had to do was get to the den, sleep until she recovered, and then figure out what in Ada-ji was going on. Wishing she had a washcloth, she pulled up her trousers.

Oh, hurt.

The flying figures were speeding right toward her like play darts finding their target. With effort, she snapped back into action. She scrambled back into the toothcar and switched its gears, knowing she couldn't compromise the one place she might have left to hide.

Turning away from where she believed the den to be, she headed in a new direction, and was stunned to see what appeared to be the end of the land beyond. Had she missed the second den also? Her mind didn't seem to be working right, ever since she left the city.

She hoped the cliff wasn't too close, as she had gone an awfully long way, but it wasn't as if she could drive toward the pursuing fairies. Except, the fairies lived over the cliff. Why was she driving toward them?

Dime, pull it together!

Ok. They're overhead so they can't see into the toothcar. She scanned around her, looking for anything that could assist her or divert them. A rocky gully had just started to form to one side, a scar in the land as if carved by the talons of a huge beast falling over the cliff beyond.

She edged her vehicle toward the gully until she was driving parallel to it, the small dropoff just to her left. She peered over the edge, hoping it wasn't deeper than it looked, and increased the speed of the car to build its momentum. Giving the toothcar's steering a hard cut to her right, she cracked open the flimsy door and squeezed through it to the left, sliding into the gully as the car continued to roll down the slow slope, moving away from her.

Her legs aching, she started running through the gully, hoping the winged pyrsi would continue to follow the car. She tripped on the loose rock, cursing as from a distance, they changed direction and came back at her again, with terrific speed, like the wind was behind them.

"Hurt, are you fairies all this stubborn?" she muttered under her breath. "Well, you're not more stubborn than me."

She ran as best as she could and searched for somewhere else to go, somewhere to hide, but they began to catch up. Grunting, she lost her focus and slid on a growing layer of rocks, slipping onto her rear. The ropes were still in their hands and their faces looked desperate, even from a distance. She thought about Dayn, and Luja, and Tum. She pictured Tum cradling furry little Agni, and Luja's warm smile. She wanted to see them again; she wanted to go home. These beings had no right to chase her this way.

She was going to go *home*.

Furious, she wasn't sure what happened, but the ground exploded in front of her, sending dirt and rocks and brush into a huge cloud. She coughed and fanned her arms, and spat the particles from her mouth.

Stumbling to her feet, she tried to get away, to use the dust as cover to remove herself, finally, from their view. She pushed ahead through the cloud of debris, unsure of her direction. Her ankle wrenched as she lost her footing again, now sliding on her back down a long hill. Her arms flailed as she reached out to grab a nearby branch, something to stop her fall. Passing the tree, she thought she'd grabbed it but instead heard a *crack* from what she hoped was the branch. Her right arm exploded with pain.

As she slid and bumped along, she couldn't see the skies through the dust cloud around her. Was she near the cliff? It was taller than the walls of Lodon; she'd never survive the fall. Unless she could stop herself, she'd die realizing she'd traveled to the one place the fairies were presumably trying to take her.

In retrospect, that didn't seem so clever.

Her last hope of survival vanished before her as she slipped a final time, whisking down a series of slopes and ledges, at first as rocky as the plains but then, as her body gained air beneath it, she felt the whipping and grasping of branches and grass. Again and again and again, she was beaten by fronds of fern and grasped by sticky webs, until she no longer acknowledged them.

She plummeted down the sloped side of the Great Cliff, too scared to cry for her own death or for Dayn, Luja, and Tum. For Da-da. She was sorry for Da-da's pain, most of all. Branches whistled as they smacked past with force, and small animals shrieked from the surrounding limbs, jumping out of her way.

Just as Dime had accepted her mistakes and made her final peace, she smashed down to the bottom of the cliff and the world stopped spinning around her.

Yet, the landing wasn't as rough as the journey to it. She fell back onto what felt like an expensive bed, though one that smelled like rot. Her arms rose above her in slow motion as her body sunk into the springy mass, and then adjusted as she bounced back to the surface. Coughing spores and dust from her mouth, she tried to brush the branches away from her face, but her limbs would not respond.

Just as the mound of decay offered her a bed of luxury, it provided a lace canopy as well. This one green, and made of layer after layer of dancing leaves. Dime blinked her eyes, as crossing boughs dotted with growth wavered in and out of her blurry vision. They extended above her in every direction, obscuring any sign of the sky. Any sign of Sol. Any sign of the cliff above.

Her head throbbed and a ringing overtook her hearing. Through her shock, she reached for her injured arm with the other, meeting a layer of warm, slick blood.

Dime had never felt blood like this before. She had never lost her sight. She had never smelled like poop. She had never seen so much green. She had never been chased by fairies. She had never fallen off a cliff. She had only left her career. Perhaps that hadn't been the best choice.

The last thing Dime remembered thinking before the pain in her limbs overtook her was, *No one will ever find me here.*

Interlude

Cel sang to herself as she cranked down the wrench. It was an old melody, but she made up new words every time. Kept things interesting.

"Yallo?" she called out, noticing a shape hovering in the doorway.

A pyr crept in, wringing xyr manicured hands and looking side to side. Cel snorted; she'd met the type before. Thought pyrsi like her were contagious.

"Fe'Cel?" xe inquired. "My, uh, car got bent up."

"Yep," Cel responded. "And you are?" Irritated her something serious; pyrsi thought just because she had a hemsa and had to work down here in the low city that common manners didn't apply. Who talks to someone without introducing xyrself? I mean, other than hand-wringer here.

"Ma' . . . Ma'To." See, that annoyed her more. *To?* He said it like he was asking her. Not his real name, then. Fine. She was used to that too.

"Look, I'm not going to ask who sent you and I don't use signed notes. But if you're looking to get a toothcar repaired, I can take care of it for you." *And at twice the speed and a tenth the rate you'd get from lawful sorts, too.* But, he already knew that or he wouldn't be here. Consorting with her kind.

The pyr's eyes caught the car she was working on and he straightened up. Circling the raised car, he ran his hands just over the top rim, respectful enough not to touch the freshly bent metal. At least he had manners for cars.

"All custom," Cel bragged. "Top of the line night in the city. Two drivers, two pass', and a thick curtain for privacy." She bent down to the wheel and tapped her nails against one of the spikes. "Sharp as needles, these. Won't bend, won't bump you around, and don't even tear up the roads. In case you got a private drive."

Cel stood and slapped her hand on the car's shoulder rod. "Full metal frame; only wood in the seats. Side doors in the back." She scowled. "I tried to get them to pay for front doors or at least a front shield, but I guess the drivers can just eat dust. I'd add them anyway, but then they'd run me for overcharging. Pyrsi down here, we can't take risks. Though—I did give 'm the smoothest pedal motion I got."

The pyr stepped back, snapping out of the car-spell that had distracted him from her hemsa. "What'd you do?" he blurted.

Cel rolled her eyes. *You could just read it; it's right here on my face.* "Got creative with some connections on gear parts. Didn't realize my sources were pouring themselves a few extra off the MC molds." Noting his confusion, she clarified. "Maintenance Circle."

"Stealing!" Ma'NotHisRealName whispered. "Stealing's like the Violence."

"Yeah, like, they didn't call it stealing since they were just borrowing the equipment. Anyway, I was wrapped up in it and now I'm down here."

Cel tried to make light of life with a hemsa, but truth told, she still hadn't adjusted. She didn't trust the pyrsi around here; some of them played a real "nothing to lose" bit and she never knew who meant it. There was always housing, and she could get whatever she needed from the freeshops. Folks thought that was enough.

Even going into the city, the best she could do was stay at street level, listening to even more clanking toothcars, like, wasn't that already her life.

It wasn't worth the glares. Not for a dipped longfruit anyway.

Though, finding a high spot to gaze at the mountains— Sometimes that was worth it.

So she made what she could and donated most of it to the freeshops.

No longer averting his eyes, the ma'pyr was downright staring at her. "Why didn't you just tell them no? To the hemsa. What . . . what could they do?" Realizing what he had suggested as his eyes shot open wide, the pyr took one longing look at Cel's mods and rushed back out into the street.

"*Killstroke,*" Cel murmured, the thought never having occurred to her.

Act 2

OVER THE CLIFF

Dime had no idea how long she'd slept in the muck, but her skin itched, her arm stung with fury, and her ankle throbbed. She smacked her tongue against the roof of her mouth in disgust, wishing she could rinse out the taste of stale blood, or the smell of her filthy clothes.

Using her less painful arm, she fumbled to twist around and feel her opposite ankle. As she suspected, it was swollen and tender. From the intense pain in her injured arm, she feared the cut ran deep. Without much medical training herself—Luja was the one with the calling—she only hoped no bones had been broken.

"Everything else will heal," her father had always said. Except it didn't, not the way the others healed. Dime's cuts always healed more slowly than her friends'; her aches lasted longer.

And this was one rockpile of injuries. It had been a while since she'd had a bruise, and now her bruises had bruises.

Letting her head loll back into the mud, she groaned, hoping some of the bugs strolling by would at least express a little sympathy. She couldn't walk with her ankle like this. But she was as thirsty as she could remember ever being, and now her stomach pinched with hunger. She couldn't stay here. Feeling like one of the kitapillars lining the branch to her side, Dime wriggled out of the maze of sticks and vines—at a dreadfully slow pace and with

the ground squishing beneath her—until she freed herself from
the tangle.

She gazed at the scenery around her. So it hadn't been a dream.
Or a nightmare. She couldn't see the cliff itself, only tall trees which
seemed to reach all the way to Sol. The light was dim, and what
reached her bounced and hopped through the layers of . . . the forest.
This was it. The Undergrowth. The land of the fairies.

All her life she had been taught to fear and avoid thoughts of this
wicked place, yet even in her beleaguered state, nothing felt wicked
in the symphony of drops, swooshes, and whispers. The richness of
the color—greener than any festival banner in Lodon—sang within
her heart. It was familiar, welcoming. This was a sacred place, and
she felt . . . robbed.

What she had been taught was at best a half-truth. Every ch'pyr
learned that these fairies, who called themselves Fo-ror, had stolen
from Sol's own creatures, the Ja-lal. Their incitement of the Violence
had nearly destroyed Ada-ji, culminating in the Great War, an event
so heinous that it was scarcely discussed beyond its existence and
consequence.

All anyone needed to know was that the Ja-lal had won, driving
the wicked fairies out of Sol's great land and into the Undergrowth,
where they stayed, wallowing in mud. That the only way to stay
the Violence was a lack of contact, of knowledge, of anything but a
hidden fear, lodged in the back of every pyr's mind.

No one had spoken of the Undergrowth's beauty. Dime questioned, even, how it was said that the Ja-lal had won. Even here, as
she wallowed in the mud herself, richness surrounded her—in the
colorful flowers, wide fronds, and the dancing of the light. Woodsy
scents intermingled, punctuated by clicks, chirps, and whirrs.

She had also been taught that the fairies were nothing like pyrsi.
That they were big-eyed with menacing screams and beast-like
manes. Over time, she'd doubted whether they even existed. Yet the
ones she had seen looked just like Ja-lal, excepting the wings and
the handsome locks of hair.

Two things, inherently false. And so, what else was false? The canopy swayed above her, as if whispering in reply.

Also, then, what was true? Was the Violence ended here, as well as in Sol's Reach? Or did it thrive? What danger was she in?

For the moment, she was alone, without sign of any pyrsi: fairy or not. Above and around her, green-covered branches creaked and swayed under the bounce of furry, chattering squips and the occasional falling fruit. Fronds and ferns entranced her with their delicate patterns and slow movement. Her hand sunk into a patch of moss, its softness welcome against her scratched fingers. The ground was as wet as Sol's Reach was dry.

The forest was quiet and loud all at once: busy yet calm. Even over the brew of rot and Dime's own epic stench, it smelled like a boutique. And, as her eyes adjusted, she saw, dotting the green, every color of those parchment sleeves that she had kept in her office drawer for all those cycles. If they really were from here—she'd assumed that was just a story—how had they even been purchased?

She'd never seen so many trees. A grim image flashed in her mind of these beautiful trees being cut and made into lumber, as had been done across Sol's Reach. Dime shivered, a protective feeling settling in. Yet lumber built homes and beds; it built the ramps and bucketpulls that allowed all pyrsi to climb the towers. It made art, and paper for learning. Sol's Reach took care of all its burgesses through building and sharing; did the fairies not care for theirs?

Called by the peaceful beauty of this vibrant land, even her feelings for the fairies—whose actions had not dispelled the teachings of their evil and greed—felt confused. Blurry. Or perhaps it was just her light head from lack of food or drink.

At this point, there was no more running left in Dime, so while she wasn't willing to give up, she conceded she had not much left to give if the fairies were to suddenly arrive. She knew she should try to move, though, at least away from where she had landed after her fall.

With a few crisp words that she hoped every forest creature

could hear, she dragged herself, a measure at a time, in what her wristpiece told her was alongside the cliff. With injured limbs and no climbing tools, she had no idea how to get back up. Her best bet now was to find a place to hide and recover.

As thirsty as she was, she resisted the urge to lick the rotting muddy water that pooled on the ground. Yet it must have come from somewhere. Dragging herself along, and listening for any signs of movement, she compromised on an old tree stump, cradling a puddle of rainwater. Forcing restraint, she ran her tongue across the small pool, not wanting to soil it with her filthy face and hands.

When it clouded with brown anyway, she gave in, splashing what was left against her face and drying herself on a soft patch of moss, not unlike the moss that grew in the city corners and tower sky alleys. Though, with her rear in the air, she was still glad no one was here to watch her do it.

Moving at a pace so slow she could hardly stand it, she thought frequently of Dayn and their children. They would tell her to stay calm, not to lose hope. They would tell her they wanted to see her again. Luja would rush to her side and tend each wound. Oh, that she could reach ver to be tended. For that goal, Dime was able to push forward, one wriggle at a time.

Ahead, she saw a cluster of red. The little dots looked just like the hackberries that decorated so many of the walls of Lodon, painted into corners and over archways with an artist's eye. But—she didn't think they were real!

Moving closer, she pulled a bunch into her reach, pulling until the branch snapped. She almost shoved every one into her mouth, but then remembered it couldn't be wise to eat a berry she had thought fictional just strides ago.

As it so often does, hunger won over wisdom, and Dime devoured several dozen of the plump berries, spitting the tiny pits to the side as the tart sweetness filled her senses. She chuckled; as tired and disoriented as she felt—if she was waiting for visions to overtake her or poison to slow her, she didn't know how she might tell the difference. Going on the convenient theory that she would be just fine, she opened her largest still-intact pouch and filled it with as many of the berries as she could reach.

As she pulled herself further, she realized that the berries were not a hidden trove, but a common feature here, as tree after tree featured clusters of the tiny but lush fruit. Only when her pouch was bulging with the red berries did she stop harvesting them each time they came into reach. Following their growth, she pushed through the vines and branches to find a trickle of water, not even a stream. She took a long drink, which, even unfiltered, tasted clean and fresh. Her thirst desperate, she ignored her concerns.

Having lost track of time and unable to see Sol clearly through the towering trees, she didn't know how far she was now from night. Night had been a long time away when she'd brought her crate back home to unpack, but it was hard to say how long she'd been riding across the plains, and how long she had stayed unconscious in the brush. Even now, she'd dragged through the forest for so long that her focus was as battered as her damaged body. And there were no bells here to reorient her.

When night fell, it might fall quickly, and Dime would be alone— without lamps, unable to see her way or treat her wounds. She could tell from the pain and blood that her arm was badly gashed. Yet, she had nothing to treat it with. She considered gathering the large leaves to provide a bandage, but she wasn't sure what she could use to tie them into place. Her pendant hung from her neck, nestled within her shirt, but she was reluctant to remove it, let alone tie wounds with it.

Oh! Ador's gift was wrapped with string. Hoping she still had it, and feeling more than emotional on the subject, she struggled to reach the side pouch it was in. After a bit of wrestling with her jacket, the package sprang free and tumbled to the ground. Cursing, she swept it up and cuddled it like the last friend she might ever see.

She imagined Ador watching over her, one eyebrow raised, waiting to see what she thought of his gift. With a chuckle, she moved to open the small package. Setting the dyed twine to one side, she pried the box open with her scratched fingers, wincing as streaks of blood smeared onto its yellow surface. She wouldn't keep the box, then.

Two small objects rolled into her palm: a dodecahedron made of solid onyx and an icosahedron made of solid amethyst. She gasped at the expertly crafted dice, twelve- and twenty-sided, with their precisely engraved symbols. As with Ador himself, Dime appreciated the many facets of his gift. And she was glad he was not here to see her weeping over the tiny objects, which in this moment seemed unquestionably thoughtful.

Sniffing back her last tears, and glad she had found the water to supply them, Dime tucked the little dice into separate pockets of her valuables pouch, sealing the little clasp. She could roll for luck later. For now, she'd have to pretend she knew how to treat her arm.

Painfully, Dime shook off her jacket. Her shirt was glued to her skin with dried blood and mud and whatever else she had rolled in, and her injuries were too severe for her to undress fully, yet she knew she needed to clean the wound. She slid her utility knife from her jacket, pulled it open, and—nervous at the blade in her unsteady hand—sawed the sleeve from her shirt.

Peeling the bloodied fabric off of her arm with gritted teeth, she was annoyed to see that the wound cut right through her best tattoo—a pattern of ice that had crystalized on her window one time during the cold season. She had drawn it out on thin paper and taken it directly to an artist. Now, a crusty swath cut through it, like the window itself had been broken.

More than the severity of the wound itself, its intrusion across the pattern of her tattoo irritated Dime's spirit back into action. To resistance. Harm it, she was going to find a way out of this forest and get back to her family. And no fairy was going to stop that.

"You hear that?" she asked the forest, hoping the fairies would get the message. "You are going to stop bothering me right now. This has been quite enough."

With caution, Dime lowered her bare arm into the stream, keeping the deepest part of the cut above water. She moved her arm in small motions, watching circles of filth spread out. Grimacing against the sting of her own touch, she ran her fingers over the broken skin, wishing she had soap or knew which plants had antiseptic properties.

Instead, she cleaned the wound as best she could with water. She snapped off a few leaves that looked large enough to serve as bandages, wrapping them around and—having to use her teeth and glad no one could see because she always chastised pyrsi who used their teeth to grip—she tied the orange string around it, keeping the wrapping snug. Finally, she drew a sharp breath. *Oww.*

As she rolled back onto a patch of soft ground cover, feeling lightheaded, her laughs broke out in bellows. "I make—the worst medic of all time. It's true," she said to a disheveled gray squip staring at her with beady black eyes and a quivering jaw. "You had to be thinking it."

After a bit, she wriggled her jacket back on and washed the piece of fabric she'd cut from her sleeve in the stream, wringing it and then threading it through a loop on her jacket to dry.

"Back to it," she declared with a forced grin.

Thoughts of her family helped push her onward as she searched for a safe place to rest. Each place she found was too rocky, too exposed, or most often too wet. Her ankle still throbbed, and she knew better than to try putting weight on it, so with her velour pants starting to tear from wearing against the ground, she edged up a hill, realizing she'd have to find a spot to rest amongst whatever was there. She was just, well, out of scooch.

As she reached the top of the hill, she found a dry enough patch in between a cluster of trees that she hoped blocked her from view. Yet, just as she leaned back against a tree and tried not to think that the leaves were probably now as stuck to her arm as her shirt had been, the shadows caught her eye in an unnatural way, falling in a grid against the brush. Grumbling, but needing to know if she was about to fall asleep in the shadow of a fairy tower, she shuffled around to the other side of the trees.

A large net rose overhead, reaching up from the ground and then spreading as far as she could see in either direction, like a massive fence. Constructed of a grid of tightly hewn rope, she could barely have pushed a fist through any of the angled openings. She tugged at the net's base, but it was secured into the dirt with long spikes.

If she had her notebook, her legs, the use of both arms, or more than a spice spoon's worth of strength, she would have explored the enigmatic structure. She would have investigated what it protected her from, or what it protected. Even if she was now a former IC agent, it was still in her nature to know.

Yet, her pants were torn, her leaf bandage was a sad excuse for medical treatment, she'd felt more pain in the last hours than she'd felt her whole life, and she wasn't even mad at herself for blatantly whining about it.

If it weren't for all that, she knew she'd be more disturbed by the large ominous fence. She also knew that she should be, but right now, her energy was focused on survival. Energy that was running out.

Crawling back toward her patch of grass, she decided this place was as safe as any she could reach, and she was best off getting some sleep. Maybe her ankle would begin to heal and she could walk again. She'd sprained hers only once before, back in her Aoch, playing ball with the other ch'pyrsi. She remembered her father telling her to stay put until it was better.

As she leaned back into the soft moss, she wished again that Luja were here. Luja would know what to do; ve always did. Even if ve didn't know, ve'd act with all the confidence in the world, daring you to doubt ver. Even more than most pyrsi vis age. And then Dime thought of Tum also. Her little child had never had legs. How unimpressed Tum would be with Dime's dilemma now. She'd tell her, *Come home, Ma-ma. Find a way.*

"I'm coming home, Tum. I'm doing my best. Tum, I've got a hug for you. Luja, you can fix my bandage. I love you. Ma-ma loves you."

Keeping her eyes open as long as she could, not knowing for certain if they would ever open again, she thought for a moment of Dayn, wishing she could show him this place—that he could join her in the shadowed glen, amongst the most spectacular sights she'd ever seen. Trunks rising to Sol verself. The songs of birds, insects, and all the furry creatures, sniffing her way while keeping their distance. Smells and whirrs and soft ground, not rocky. So soft it required no mat.

As she drifted into an exhausted and painful sleep, Dime began to have the strangest dream—of a screeching noise, and of wide, scaly arms cradling her and carrying her away.

Content, Dime snuggled into the warm chest, the softness of its feathers a welcome rest.

Dime awoke to great number of alarming changes. She fought back pangs of terror at the feel of sand in her fingers. Her first thought was that the fairies had found her after all. Her second thought was that she was completely naked. Her third thought was that a huge rough tongue was licking the side of her neck.

Sitting up with an involuntary yelp that caused the tongue to withdraw, Dime was enveloped by the complete and unyielding darkness around her. Sick from the pain still permeating her body, she wanted to escape, but had no information to aid her. Where was she; which way was out?

Calm, calm, calm, she urged herself. *Gather facts.*

Naked she was, though relief flashed through her as she found her diamond pendant still in place, as was her compass wristband. Catching her breath and swatting helplessly in the direction of the tongue—the huge tongue could not be underplayed—she gathered what information she had.

She was not dead; whether or not one believed in an afterlife, this was not it. She had been placed on a mound of fine sand, perhaps like a bed. Her injured arm was caked in dried mud, and the tongue had been wildly disgusting, but not unkind. So, something was caring for her, and she had a pretty good idea it was not the fairies. In the stories she'd been told about the fairies, they had flown like bugs, wielded their valence, and selfishly hoarded the forest.

There had been no stories about licking in dark caves. Thank Sol.

The pain had not subsided much, but at least her mind felt a little clearer now. She squeezed her ankle. It was smaller and less tender, though not healed. It would be foolish still to put any weight on it. The pain from her arm was dulled a bit, though she wasn't sure what a glop of mud was going to do to it. And, she surmised, the creature that watched her now could probably see in the dark. Shapes began to form in Dime's vision, but she could not make them out.

At this point, Dime really missed her home. But, as she had always told her children, there were times in life where the only way out was through.

"Hello," she offered, working to keep her voice calm. "Thank you for your help. I am scared here in the dark. Can we go outside?" A weight shuffled in the sand but did not otherwise respond. Dime reminded herself that the being could see. She tried again.

She waved toward the large shape in front of her and then to her own eyes. "I can't see in the dark." She pointed away. "Please, take me where I can see." She pointed to her eyes, and this time moved her hands about in different directions, hoping to illustrate her dilemma.

Forcing terror back down her throat, she tried not to make any sudden moves as the large shape shuffled toward her, and then a pair of large arms picked her up and carried her away. Yes, she remembered now. These same arms had taken her from the glen. They were smooth, with scales like a lizard. Larger than a pyr's arms and notably stronger. And yet, soft feathers tickled at her from the side. Scales and feathers?

Newts! Dime's threshold for what she was willing to consider had dropped substantially throughout the latter part of this turn, as the only creatures that she had grown up being taught to fear more than the wicked, flying fairies were the grotesque and primitive newts that shared their lands.

Depicted as monsters in tales meant to teach ch'pyrsi good behavior, it had not taken Dime much convincing to avoid thinking of the unruly beasts. Her teachers used to warn their young students that the newts might eat their mid-lesson meals if they didn't finish them, but even then, Dime had thought they were a parable, exaggerated for effect. By instinct, she struggled, but the arms held her close.

A soft breeze met them as the light of the skystones revealed a barren field. It was night now, so she must have slept, or even fallen unconscious, for a long time. If being cradled in a newt's arms wasn't enough of a shock, the complete change of scenery floored her. She couldn't imagine where this place was. It bore no resemblance to her former perception of the Undergrowth nor to what she had seen herself in its tall, green forest.

But she knew Sol's Reach from corner to corner, and this was not in Sol's Reach. Where was she?

The landscape gained detail as her eyes adjusted to the diffused nightlight. The field extended from the edge of a vast body of water, its waves gently lapping against a sandy beach. Large burrows were dug into the sand, fortified by mud and sticks and debris, creating an orderly row of bumps, each more than a stone's throw apart. Away from the water, she saw a large stretch of mostly flat land fading into a dark horizon.

Dime had never seen the edge of the land before, nor the great Sha that surrounded it. Sol's Reach was bordered on the nor and to the eas by mountains of increasing height and severity. While most speculated that they didn't truly go on without end, there were limits to how far pyrsi could travel before the conditions became too harsh. To the sur loomed the cliff beyond which the fairies lived.

The wes was the only potential path to the edge of Ada-ji, but it was flanked by a series of steep, tree-covered ledges known as the dark woods, for which the dangers and general superstitions were so great as to prevent the Ja-lal, thus far, from exploring the area or harvesting the old trees that grew within it. A few adventurers, though, had reported it ended directly at the Sha, with stunning cliffs against which the waves crashed and churned.

As certain as she could be that this land was nowhere in the borders of Sol's Reach, she had to assume that she was on some edge of the Undergrowth. And these—they must be newts.

The arms nestled Dime into the sand, shifting her back and forth as if stabilizing a shaped rock within a sand garden. The large figure moved around to her front, plopping down across from her. As Dime's eyes adjusted further to the dim light, they fell on a creature resting patiently in the sand, stabilized by its long arms. Bulky and muscular, it was at least half again as large as a tall pyr, and covered with feathers, their ruffled outline tracing the nightlight.

The newt stared at her with an expectant gaze.

"Hello," Dime said. She pointed at her own quite bare chest. "Fe'Dime. Er, Fe'Diamond. I am honored to meet you." She felt a sense of formality, as if making an introduction on behalf of her kind.

The feathery newt, who appeared of female sex, reached forward and rubbed Dime's chest. Dime tried not to jump. "No, no," she corrected, leaning back, and almost falling over before balancing back up with her stronger arm. Trying again, she pointed at her chest. "Dime."

She reached toward the newt's chest, noting what looked like a shawl of white feathers over the darker colors that covered the rest of her body. Darker lines sprung from her shoulders. In the darkness, they looked like sprigs of dried juniper. The hardy plants were popular in Lodon; she was surprised they grew here also.

Dime pointed at the newt's chest, then looked up inquiringly. The newt seemed to understand, as it bounced in place, responding with a combination of moans and clicks. Dime made exactly one attempt to replicate the animal's name, which she thought started with some sort of a *ja* sound. Whatever she did say appeared to cause some offense, so Dime motioned toward the dark sprigs. "These are beautiful. Juniper, right? Can I call you Juni?" she asked. "Juni?"

The newt appeared to shrug, so Dime decided she'd go with that, repeating "Juni" with a smile. Juni clicked and chortled, shuffling around to caress Dime's back. Dime was certainly not resolved to all this ungranted touching, but she could concede Juni acted as though it was all completely normal. Dime tried not to overreact.

That said, it was hard to stay calm as Juni *oohed* and *aahed* over Dime's exposed back. Dime liked to keep her back covered, as a large feathery tattoo swept across the breadth of it and onto one shoulder, concealing large scars that she'd had as long as she could remember. Something to do with her birth, Da-da had said. She could now add to them what was sure to be a whopping scar on her arm.

"Ok, that's enough," Dime said with a shudder. "And they aren't feathers, as you can see. Just feathery tattoos. Which feels a little awkward with you here. So. Do you have my clothes?" With her uninjured arm, Dime patted around her body. "My clothes?"

Juni puzzled over this a bit, then grinned, dipping back into her burrow and returning with a heap of fabric.

After Juni's efforts to undress Dime for cleaning, what was left of her soft velour work clothes was too torn and tattered to be worn, even as a drape. At least she'd have a pillow, once she washed it all out. For some shred of modesty, Dime slipped on her jacket with its pouches, then pulled the clean-ish piece of cut fabric from its loop and made herself an awkward, well, thong. It was better than nothing. Dime tried to ignore the gleam of her protruding hips in the nightlight and the sparkle of her pendant against her mostly bare chest.

"I'm glad you don't have mirrors here," Dime said to Juni. "I'm sure I look like a Ba-ji dancer!" With a grimace, Dime added,

"Ok, not quite. It was in theory. They are really great, if you ever get the chance."

Juni cocked her head, seeming distressed by Dime's words. Though she'd thought of it more as talking to herself, Dime considered how left out she'd feel if someone made a joke she didn't understand. Dime resolved to stick to ideas familiar to the newt, just in case Juni could glean intent from her tone and gestures.

To avoid stressing her right arm, and thinking the newts probably weren't as particular about which arm was used for which gestures, she placed her left fingers over her heart. "Thank you, Juni, for saving me."

She wished she had something to give the newt, then remembered the berries in her pouch. Juni's eyes sprung open as she saw Dime's hand fumble with the latch. "You know what's in here, don't you?" The newt had ample opportunity to have taken the berries, and she had not.

An unsettled feeling grew in Dime's gut, as she imagined all the scores of Ja-lal ch'pyrsi being taught to fear and avoid these creatures. This one, at least, seemed compassionate and warm, if a bit intimate.

Juni clicked and jumped in circles before extending her arms as if to pick Dime back up. As hungry as she was, Dime left the hackberries alone for the moment and leaned in toward Juni's grasp. *At least that was almost like permission.* Juni swept her back up and carried her off. The newt broke into a run, and Dime pushed back her nerves, at least feeling secure in the newt's strong grasp.

They ran past a dozen or two burrows and toward a flat area under a large rocky overhang, where Dime could see several shapes emerging in the darkness.

A group of newts gathered under the ledge, ceasing all activity as she and Juni approached. In the dim light, it was hard to make them out exactly, but Dime peered and gleaned as much as she could.

Shapes dotted the wide gathering area, perhaps mud and sticks to form seating places. Sticks leaned against the side facing the beach, roughly interwoven with twigs. She supposed that served to block the winds she'd felt coming from over the large water surface. From Sha. There was no fire, or any traces of one. The air smelled salty, but clean, lacking the musty smells of the forest, the dusty air of the plains, or the mixed odors of Lodon.

The beach was quiet, without the rustling of plants or scurrying of small animals. Only the waves rose up onto the beach like a slow pulse.

Like Juni, the other newts were all much larger than pyrsi. They stared at her with large, dark eyes, set atop a strong, squarish bone structure centered by a small nose. Their wide mouths bore a range of expressions, not all of which Dime knew how to interpret. Juni sat her down on the edge of the gathering.

The newts' scaly limbs shone in the nightlight, from their mid-biceps down to their pronounced claws, long and pointy like the spikes of a toothcar. Long feathers surrounded their bare, pale faces and covered their shoulders, chests, and backs. With the others mostly dark in color, Juni's white feathers stood out among them.

If Dime could gauge age, for without darkening skin she had to go on more subtle elements like facial wrinkles and posture, Juni seemed to be among their youngest. And, as if reacting to a curious ch'pyr in Dime's own city, the elders did not look so pleased at what she had brought. Dime hoped she could help the young newt out.

"Thank you," Dime said, taking the effort this time to raise her casted arm, as best she could, to her heart. She tapped the mud cast with her other arm. "You saved my life."

Dime could make no sense of the chorus of arguments that erupted. Her eyes were drawn, as Juni's seemed to be also, to the oldest of the group. The creature's eyes were stern, unyielding. Dime had met pyrsi like this before. And Dime knew not to underestimate them.

Crawling toward Stern Eyes, as she'd subconsciously nicknamed the female newt, Dime detached the pouch laden with berries, opening it and dumping them onto the ground, in between the gathered newts. Seeing what she had done, the others hushed. Dime clipped the empty pouch back onto her jacket.

Stern Eyes nodded. Then, as if unable to contain herself, the elder rolled the berries across the sand, surveying them. She let a quick howl, yet no newts approached. Soon, others in the camp, or village—Dime wasn't sure what to call it—joined them, and only then did everyone rush for the pile.

Juni nudged her forward, and Dime again tried not to get spun up about all the pushing and touching. Reaching for the berries, Dime hungrily ate what seemed like a reasonable share. The newts ate the seeds, but Dime wasn't going to risk that. Teeth didn't get stronger with age, she'd learned the hard way a couple times already. Dime hoped they'd forgive her as she spat the small pits off to the side. No one seemed to mind or even notice.

It was obvious that there was no feast awaiting her here. No fire, no warm table laden with mashed roots or savory stew. The newts appeared to be as starving as Dime was, though not just over the last turn, as was Dime's case. "You're hungry," Dime whispered to Juni, patting her own stomach.

Juni growled and raced off. Perhaps she had understood that just fine. When Juni returned, she held in her hand a fragment of ropes, a small piece of the massive netting Dime had encountered in the forest. The way she held it was like poison, and her face reflected the same.

Then the netting was for the newts . . . to keep them out of the forest, perhaps? Maybe Juni had been trying to find a way through. She did have that spirit of a young agent about her. Of discovery and justice. To Dime, it was familiar.

Yet, she had not taken Dime's berries when certainly she must have found them. It rang of honor, of fairness. Dime felt guilty assessing them this way, passing judgment on their traits as though judgment were hers to assign. Just bells ago, she still believed newts to be dangerous animals, in league with the fairies. Yet, the fairies had tried to capture her, and—

Dime yelped as Juni lifted her jacket from behind, showing Stern Eyes her exposed back. "Hey!" Dime exclaimed, spinning around. "No!" She stopped at the alarmed look in the older newt's eyes. Stern Eyes spoke to Dime with quiet intensity, yet Dime could not understand any of the sounds. Dime raised her arm in confusion, and Stern Eyes stopped, seeming to understand. Or, to understand that Dime did not.

Stern Eyes grabbed the fragment of net, slamming it onto the sand. Like kneading the toughest seitan into a dein, she slammed it down, again and again, pointing to Dime. "Yes, the fairies," Dime confirmed. "They tried to capture me." Dime made a flying motion, like wings, miming pursuit. Then she reenacted her own feelings, making a face of fear and motioning as though she were trying to get away.

Grabbing a loose stick, she traced a picture of the mountains into the sand, and the towers rising at their base. Of Lodon. And pointed to herself. "Ja-lal," she said. She tapped the sketch of tiny Lodon. "Lodon." And back to herself. "Ja-lal."

Several of the beings pulled back their lips and screeched, in what Dime read as a form of laughter. Stern Eyes silenced them with a gesture and a glare. Or mostly, as a few *tsks* lingered. Stern Eyes snapped something at Juni. Dime wondered if it was the newt equivalent of, "see me later." Dime wondered what she'd said that hadn't translated, but she kept her mouth shut for the moment, not wanting to exacerbate whatever had transpired between the newts.

As if to apologize, Juni jumped to Dime's side, licking the side of Dime's leg in careful swatches. Dime winced at the rough surface against her cuts.

"Oh! It's ok," she said, giving Juni a look she hoped read as gratitude. But the licking was not going to be a part of their continued relationship. Maybe reading Dime's lean to the side, for Dime hoped she wasn't smelling her emotions or something, Juni stood back up.

With another look at Stern Eyes, Juni swept Dime into her arms—of course without permission—and raced off across the sandy reaches of this place Dime had not known to exist, leaving behind them an intense chatter from the gathered newts.

First, they ran to the water. Awed by what seemed an endless span of blackness painted with fluffy white ripples, Dime thought she'd never pry her eyes away. Juni tipped Dime down toward the edge of the shiny surface, enabling her to take a drink.

Dime tasted the water, remembering that Sha's water was supposed to contain more minerals than that from the mountains and the rain. Spitting and gasping, Dime recoiled, unable to drink the salty, strong water, which pinched at her throat and constricted her breathing.

No other communication was necessary as Juni seemed to realize Dime's dilemma. She uttered a series of animated clicks before setting Dime down in the sand. Digging her claws into the ground, she leaned in for a long drink, the strong water not bothering the large, feathery newt. Juni paused in silence, as if in reverence to the water itself, and then shook the excess water from her lips.

With a few more clicking sounds, Juni scooped Dime from the sand, and off they raced again. This time they ran a long way, Dime continuing to wonder how such broad expanses of barren land could exist outside of Ja-lal knowledge and how the newts could survive here. If she ever got back home, she wanted to find a way to help.

But Dime was in no state to help anyone, she thought with a laugh, as she had no idea where she even was, couldn't leave, and still had no idea why she'd been pursued in the first place.

"What a mess," she muttered. Juni responded with something that sounded like understanding.

Even in the darkness, Dime could see the terrain becoming rougher and shrubbier as they ran. After what felt like a few takes, they started uphill, and the silhouettes of tall trees emerged into view.

Juni didn't slow down much as she reached the trees. Dime, only slightly embarrassed, snuggled into her chest in fear of the branches and grasses whipping by.

They stopped so suddenly that Dime was convinced for a stride she would fly out like a fairy. With relief to still be in Juni's steady grip, she was lowered next to a small puddle. Though it appeared clean, she tried not to think about the unfiltered water as she cupped her hand in and drank. She stared at the small puddle, not enough for a village.

Dime pointed up into the trees. "Fo-ror?" she asked. The newt's feathers poofed out on both sides. "I'm sorry," Dime corrected. "I didn't mean to upset you. They're keeping you away, aren't they?" *Odd, they seem to want me just fine.*

Juni ran several paces away and began scratching her claws downward with great speed and force, throwing up a spray of dirt until there was a sizable hole. Dime scooted back, curious. Then, the newt stuck her head in the hole. And stayed there. Now, Dime had no idea what to do in this situation, but she tried to imagine her own hurt, having been touched only once by the Fo-ror, and not living with family who starved for seasons on end. She visualized the large net. She wondered how close they were to it now.

Scooting over, Dime reached out toward Juni's large shape. With caution, for she'd been raised not to touch animals unless they approached her, she rested a hand on the newt's broad back. Sensing no discomfort, she began to stroke the long, soft feathers back into place. It wasn't too long before Juni's feathers settled back, and she lifted her face from the hole. "I'm sorry," Dime offered. "You explore this place, don't you? For food? Maybe for a way through?"

Her expression for a moment taking on the hard quality of Stern Eyes' own, Juni motioned up the hill, making a terse sound that Dime was certain meant the Fo-ror. She tried to remember the sound.

With an occasional grunt or click, Juni took to sniffing around the area where Dime sat, digging around with her long, sleek talons. Thinking of the hole Juni had made so quickly, Dime considered why they didn't dig under the net. They seemed accustomed to burrowing, though she hadn't seen them tunnel.

Several trees away, Juni tugged on a long stalk until a tapered root popped out. She moved to eat it but instead offered it out to Dime. Unsure of the protocol, Dime rubbed it with her hands to remove the loose dirt and then took a bite. She'd prefer it cooked, but it had a sweet and mild taste she enjoyed. She handed the rest back to Juni, who crunched it down, stalk and all, in one big bite.

Oh! Dime detached the pouch that had held the berries. She opened it and held it steady as Juni poked and sniffed the fabric. Juni hesitated, so Dime set the pouch down and mimed pulling a root and putting it in the bag. It took Juni a bit to understand, but Dime stayed patient, repeating the motions. With a squeal, Juni snatched the pouch away and ran off, not returning until it was bulging with the pointy root.

Dime wasn't too upset—just this once—when Juni ran her rough tongue up the side of Dime's face. "Ok, ok," she scolded, chuckling. "That's enough."

Dime rested dozens of time over the next two turns, her battered body craving the additional sleep. Juni tended to her like a nurse: carrying her to wash in the water or relieve herself, and then back to the burrow when there was a wind.

As Sol's light had first illuminated her surroundings upon the arrival of day, Dime took in not just the unusual landscape, but the colors that had not shown themselves to her in the dark.

The newts' colors were her first surprise. Their faces were a light lavender rather than gray, complementing the dark shades of their scales. With some variations, and a few of those stark, like her friend's collar of white, the newts bore long, regal feathers that ranged from brown or tan to the richest shades of purple, some even tinged with hints of orange, yellow, or red. Their palette struck her as lusher and more elegant than any Lodon mural. A few wove dried leaves or vines across their chests, though none with as much flair as Juni's shoulder sprigs.

The next surprise was the love that went into what she had presumed to be simple animal burrows. Each was constructed differently, some with patterns of bark and sticks forming the entrance, as elegant in their context as the structural towers of Lodon.

Inside the front of each, where light streamed in during the daytime, trinkets were stuck into the packed mud walls. Juni's trinkets were especially eclectic. Dried leaves, patterns of juniper berries, fragments of glass, colorful water-worn stones. She even wove in fragments of fabric—light airy fabrics that Dime could only suppose had been torn from fairy garments as they walked, or she supposed, flew, through the prickly trees.

Juni was as interesting as her burrow. Dime had finally set boundaries about the licking, and Juni had seemed to at least learn to live with the offense. Yet, she had no concern with carrying the wounded fe'pyr around. And so Dime, feeling a bit odd in the big feathery youth's arms but enjoying the changes in scenery, let the newt carry her around their sandy beaches, in and out of the other newts' burrows, and sometimes as far as the outer edge of the forest.

Some of the newts avoided her, and others became friends. One male even taught her a game. It was mostly pushing a stick around, and Dime wasn't sure who won any particular match, but it made the newts laugh and also passed the time.

The dark nights were illuminated only by the skystones and their faint reflection off the water, but it did not lessen the newts' activity. Unused to being in the darkness without lamps, Dime was glad that her eyes continued to adjust and that she could get by well enough. Still, she was glad each time daylight returned.

The bells rolled on this way in a relative state of calm, though of course there were no literal bells here, which was a calming though disorienting change. In all the time she now had, her thoughts gravitated back to her family—and of course to the traumatic and surreal circumstances that had led her away from them.

Still, even in the calm of sitting and watching the waves travel, she could not fathom any reason why she was here. She'd spent her whole life knowing vaguely that the Fo-ror existed, but in such a distant context that they were in a different reality, if in reality at all. Characters in a story. There were moments when she wondered if she could have gone on an IC mission, been injured, and now was suffering a loss of memory. She'd read two books with that same plot.

Except this explanation was the furthest from the truth. She had nothing *but* memory on the subject. The rough touch of the fairy, the stunning luminescence of xyr wings unfurling, the pain in Dime's chest as her breath pumped too hard as she tried to escape, and the dust in her dry mouth as she rode across the plains.

In some sense she was concerned that she had not yet fully processed the events, to measure her own well-being against such shock and change. Yet there was no sense in pondering whether it could be possible—whether this could all have happened, when she knew that it had. And now, unable to walk and her arm still encased in hard mud, Dime could not imagine what any of this was about: why they had approached her, and why now.

It was time to start figuring it out.

Her ankle was tender but correctly sized; she almost felt she could try walking on it again, though she knew pushing too fast would set her back even more. Luja had taught her that, at least. She intended to wait just a little longer. But not much.

As for her arm, she considered taking off the mud, but without anything better to treat it or even filtered water to wash it properly, she held off at least until she decided to leave. Sol had risen many bells ago; perhaps she would be wiser to wait through the next night.

Damp and cold from the constantly blowing Sha breeze, barely sustained by the meager rations the newts generously shared with her, and constantly thirsty from relying on Juni to take her to fresh water, Dime could not stay here this way. Perhaps, if she were well, she could construct a home, build a fire, and scavenge for food. But she was not well, and she missed her family.

Her biggest worry wasn't their safety, for she had great trust in Dayn's abilities. But she knew they would be worried about her. Whatever the fairies were up to, she didn't think they would get word back to the Ja-lal that Dime had fallen off of the cliff and was probably dead. But she didn't know. She had no clue regarding their motivations in any of this. In fact, believing now that they were keeping the newts from the richness of the forest, Dime's resentment of the winged pyrsi grew.

As long as she stayed here, Dime had time to think. And it wasn't just frustration toward the Fo-ror that grew. All her cycles in the IC, monitoring the conduct of Ja-lal citizens in the name of peace, and there had been an entire second civilization of pyrsi living just beyond their boundaries. They hadn't studied them, asked about them, even assessed them from a distance. Their eyes averted, they lived their lives focusing on the greatness of their own society, with their neighbors reduced to whispers and superstitions. To lore.

She'd brought up researching the fairies once at the far-sur den, the second one she'd been trying to reach before she fell. The reaction to even a mention of the beings had been so swift, so horrified, that she'd not brought them up again, and back in the safety of Lodon with deadlines, management, and other projects on her mind, the idea had faded.

Back in the towers, sentiments on the subject had been clear. Any contact, it was said, would return the Violence to Ada-ji. That was just the nature of the fairies. Well, the fairies had returned anyway. And now what? The Ja-lal were wholly uninformed. Wholly unprepared. If one believed the fairies were a real threat, then what sort of strategy was this, and—most difficult to consider—why had no one questioned it?

The Free Winds. Ador's organization, the Free Winds—they had questioned it. She had heard this in rumors, that they talked openly of the fairies, of reaching out to them. Working in the Circles, Dime and Dayn could not become involved with such a controversial organization. Despite their close friendship with

Ador, Dime had not asked much, and Ador had never pressed. The fallacy of Dime's thoughts struck her like a cold wind, and a sick feeling grew in her gut.

How have I been so ignorant? So controlled?

She was eager to talk to Ador when she returned home. That said, she had no idea how to even start returning to Lodon. Her compass didn't seem to be working right, but she could at least tell nor and sur from the shadows.

Perhaps the cliff might have some sections she could climb more easily than others, but she didn't enjoy the idea of searching on her own without supplies or a toothcar for Sol knew how long to see if she could find a way back. And, she had to admit to herself, crossing Ada-ji in a tattered jacket and thong rattled every one of her Ja-lal sensitivities, regardless of what the newts didn't think about it.

Dime, so recently considered for Light's Circle! She laughed aloud, picturing Sala seeing her now. Besides being mostly naked with her arm crusted in mud, pinpricks of white *hair* had started to grow in across her scalp, peeking through her tattoos. No, by the time Sala was done ordering her to shave, Dime wouldn't be able to count her hemsa while on her way to some outer ring or outlaw village.

Well, harm that. And Sala wasn't here.

But, a tall figure walked across the sandy land. Dime blinked. The figure was still there. Dime's instincts kicked in and she realized she should either be running toward the lone figure or running away from xem. Her ankle as it was, though, she sat there. And waited. The dice would fall where they would, this time.

As the figure approached, Dime could see with relief that xe was not a fairy. No wings protruded from xyr back nor was there any cloak or wrap that could conceal them, as her pursuers had worn. Nor was it Sala, as absurd as that would have been.

The figure appeared to start, seeing Dime sitting alone in the sand. The pyr turned, heading straight her way. Feeling a bit silly, Dime waved.

The pyr was Ja-lal, but without prominent markings indicating class or status. Xe wore a simple tunic, with a large drooping bag slung across on a wide strap. Xyr tattoos were fallen leaves, each of a different level of clarity and wear, a sign of age. Dime guessed xe was a Dorh, one epoch older than Dime, by the grace in xyr walk and the darkening color of xyr skin. No hemsa marked xyr face, not that Dime was prejudiced by such things. The pyr drew near.

.   "Fe'Ella," she offered, fanning her fingers in greeting.

Dime fanned the only fingers she had available. "Fe'Dime." After that, she wasn't sure what to say. The circumstances were, after all, quite odd. Yet there was something familiar about Ella, with the small leaves over her cheekbones and the draping scarf around her neck. Dime didn't think she had seen her before.

Shifting in the sand, Dime glanced around, nervous that Juni would pop in and startle the visitor.

Ella's eyes rested on Dime a moment: her face, her necklace, and her jacket. Probably noting Dime's discomfort, she was polite enough not to look further.

"You've put yourself in a whole bucket of pickles, haven't you?" Ella shook her head, letting the large bag thump down onto the sand.

"What?" Dime's mind was racing, trying to figure out who this was while not being distracted by self-consciousness regarding her own now almost disintegrating thong. Ella appeared to read her mind.

"Hey, I brought clothes. Wasn't sure of your size so they're generic. And we'll need to knock that mud off and check your arm. They know some basics here and it probably held you over, but I brought bandages and balm. Splints if we need them, but I'm hoping we don't." Ella started to rummage through the bag then paused. "Glad to see you're clean, anyway. You never know how they'll take to pyrsi. And I sure don't blame them."

Ella chuckled, looking Dime over. "Someone has taken a right fascination to you, hasn't xe?"

"Uh, I call her Juni. She's got a band of light feathers." Dime gestured to her own shoulders.

"Oh!" Ella exclaimed. "The little one. Yes, perfect. What did the leader think of it?"

Dime squinted. "Er, Stern Eyes? I mean, I call her that. She seems to be going with it. They had some sort of talk after they laughed at me that first time, so Juni mostly keeps me away from the group area."

"Laugh? Hmm—" Ella mused while pulling out some plain garments. "Doesn't sound like them. Oh! Here she comes. Ooh," she added. "Let me knock that gunk off now; I don't want her getting protective about it."

"Yes, I'm worried that it's—"

Juni picked up speed and screeched as she saw Ella cracking at the dried mud with a handpick. Ella spun around and made a slow noise, like a cooing sound. Juni stopped, and plopped onto the sand with a face that looked just like a ch'pyr's pout. Barking out a few sounds of her own including something about the Fo-ror, Juni quieted and stared off at the sky. Ella paused, and several strides passed before she turned back around.

"Does she understand you?" Dime asked.

"I get by," was all Ella said, as she poured water over Dime's bare, shriveled, arm. Dime winced, seeing that while Juni had cleaned it within reason, there was a film of pus over the wound, as she had feared. "I don't think it's broken," Ella said under her breath, as if talking to herself.

Juni continued to pout as Ella cleaned, treated, and wrapped Dime's arm, then turned away as Dime abandoned her makeshift undergarment for good, thankful for the clean set that included a snug breast wrap.

Feeling better already, she slipped on an adjustable tunic and a baggy pair of pants. They were a simple cotton, lighter in both texture and color than her preferred dark velour suits, but after her bout of unintended nakedness they looked as fine as one of Sala's designer suits. She'd never been so grateful.

Dime flushed as she rolled up the cuff of each leg. She tried not to be self-conscious about her height, but comments from pyrsi over the cycles had made her wary.

"I don't wear heels," Dime said. "Never have. I'm the way I was made I guess." *Why am I explaining myself?*

Ella looked like she had something to say.

"What?" Dime asked.

"Nothing for now. Except, our friend here, she's feeling a touch left out." Ella shuffled over to Juni's side, giving her a huge lick across the face and scratching her neck. Dime winced, but Juni rumbled in delight.

Dime watched in astonishment as Ella and Juni had a whole conversation in moans and clicks and gestures. Some of the words almost sounded like language, while others were strictly newt. Dime started to wonder if every turn she lived now was destined to get more bizarre, like *Tale of the Winding Tunnel* or some such nonsense.

Now, Dime wished she had asked Ella a few questions when she first arrived, rather than gape at her and flush about being naked. Maybe like "Who are you?" or "Why are you here?" or "Can you promise you aren't in league with the fairies?" But, she trusted Juni. So, then.

Wanting continued use of its pouches, she reached for her now grubby work jacket and wrenched it over her soft, clean clothes. Oh, her arm felt better in the soft and flexible bandage. She tested the motion of her arm, moving it side to side with some stiffness. It seemed fine, so long as the wound continued to heal. Content, she turned back to Ella.

"Do you have any idea what's going on? With me?"

"Not very much," Ella answered.

Not very? But, oh!

"The witch of the woods!" Dime exclaimed. Ella rolled her eyes so effectively it was as if they had just orbited Ada-ji. But, wasn't that where she had heard the description? Leaves, scarves, and a curved wood staff. The mysterious witch who lived on the edge of the untouched forest, hexing anyone who passed near.

Ch'pyrsi were told that the Circles had planted her there to ward the fairies away. Dime, working in the Circles, knew there was no such thing and had dismissed all of it as a false, though persistent, story.

Dime was going to have to start taking stories more seriously.

Though, she noticed, Ella didn't have a staff. And from Ella's reaction, Dime had struck a nerve.

"Lovely," Ella snapped in a tone that set Dime back.

"I'm sorry," Dime offered. "It just . . . came to mind. Honestly, Ella, I have no idea what's happened. I have no idea why I'm here or what happens now." Trust or no trust, she was *tired*. Dime spilled everything like a guilty ch'pyr.

"I was at home and the fairies burst into my living room from the outer stairwell, I guess through the window, so no one would see them in the tower. I don't know about fairies, so I have no idea how they know about me. They tried to touch or take me or something, to give me a rest, and I got away." She watched for Ella to react, but her expression stayed blank. "They chased me over the plains and I got too close to the cliff, and—" Dime remembered with a twinge of discomfort the huge explosion that had obscured her view "—I fell over the cliff and hurt my arm and foot.

"Then I was saved by newts, who, I'm sure you know, I'd heard as much good about as the fairies, and Juni here, well—" Dime looked over to see the newt's face wrinkled with concern at Dime's distressed tone. "Ella, she saved me. I hope you can tell her how grateful I am. And if you can help me, I need to go back to Sol's Reach. I can't draw the fairies back to Lodon, but I also can't let my family continue to worry. If you can get me back to Sol's Reach, I can take it from there."

Ella finally shook her head and let a huge sigh, causing Juni to jump back. "It's a lot, Dime. I don't know, myself. Let's get you out of here and we'll sort it all out. Try to, anyway. That witch business too. But first, our friends." She threw a wave and a few sounds at Juni, who seemed annoyed as she swooped Dime up into the air.

"Whoops! Careful!" Dime reprimanded. Juni ignored the caution and ran off at full speed with Dime in her arms, leaving Ella to pick up the rest of her things.

The other newts had already gathered as Juni ran screaming toward them. She and Stern Eyes conversed with such speed and intensity that she doubted Ella could have understood it. When they were done, everyone sat back and waited.

Stern Eyes picked her teeth with a reed, not looking anywhere near Dime. Dime, however, was cradled tightly in Juni's arms, not much able to move.

"Juni," she whispered. "Friends. We are friends." Dime smiled up at her as best she could.

Juni's grip relaxed, and she placed one of her hands over Dime's chest. Dime felt a sensation in her heart. A strange feeling, as if she were touched by Juni's love, reaching out past a wall of anger. Juni removed her hand, uttering a sound that sounded a lot like, "friend." Still touched by her unexpected wave of emotion, Dime realized how true that was.

A couple of takes later, Ella appeared in the distance, lugging the bag over her shoulder without anything close to either hurry or concern. Dragging the bag up, she left it behind her as she walked under the overhang, right to where Stern Eyes was seated.

Ella motioned away from where they sat, adding a slow series of noises. Dime heard the word for Fo-ror. Ella nodded, and pointed again in the direction Dime believed to be back toward her home, the land of the Ja-lal. Stern Eyes finally turned her gaze to Dime, who was certain she was being assessed. She couldn't guess for what. Ella pointed toward Dime and cooed.

Stern Eyes broke her stare and responded to Ella with agitated clicks and a narrowed face. Wheezing, Juni rushed forward and set her down in front of Ella. Dime's rear bumped onto the ground, and Dime was glad she at least had clothes now. "Hey," she murmured. "Careful with the pyr. I've only got one butt." One of the newts chortled.

Juni continued her heavy breathing and Dime tried to offer her a smile. Juni wasn't looking.

Ella spoke again with the newts, and one ran off, returning with a long water-worn tree branch. Ella inspected it, tapping it against the ground. "Hmm," she conceded, handing it to Dime. "I think you can walk with this. Just go slow and we'll rest when needed."

Dime stood cautiously, leaning against the large staff. Though it was stiff, she was surprised to feel less pain in her ankle; it seemed to be much better. "Thank you," she said to the newt who had found the stick. He bobbed and bared his teeth in response.

Noticing Juni's distress, a knot turned in Dime's heart. She had grown up being told that the newts were the most dangerous of all animals. Frightening. Unworthy. And here, this friend had saved her, and would save her again if she had the chance.

Dime wanted to thank her. An idea struck, and she hobbled over to the young newt. "Here, for you. For your burrow." Dime found the jade lizard she'd tucked into her jacket and held it out, as smooth and translucent as when it had been given to her by her old Circlemate. "They say it's for wisdom. I don't know; you seem pretty wise. But, well. For you."

With a squeal, Juni said nothing Dime could interpret as a goodbye but instead ran off, not toward the water but toward the forest. Around them, other newts stomped and grunted.

"Extra pickles," Ella muttered.

"What?" Dime whispered.

"In a few," the older fe'pyr murmured.

With a few more words to Stern Eyes, Ella and Dime set off in a new direction, one Dime hoped would lead to Sol's Reach.

"So what was that last part?" Dime asked.

"Oh, the gift? You recognized the cub as leader of the troop."

Dime stopped, wobbling on her staff. "Wait? Was that an insult to Stern Eyes?"

Ella looked as if she'd said something absurd. "It certainly wasn't a compliment."

"Then we're going back! Come on. Stern Eyes is the only reason they didn't sail me away on Sha; we aren't leaving this way. What else do we have? That I could offer?" Ella stood and stared. "There's got to be something that's better." Ador's gift was off the table if there was any other option. And she didn't think Stern Eyes would understand her compass.

"Ok. We have our food for the way back," Ella said in monotone. "I get grumpy when I'm hungry myself, but I do see your point. Anyway, we can restock at the Crossing. We'll make it work."

Dime shook off a vague idea of what a crossing might be, as her eyes lit up at the sight of Ella's huge shoulder-strapped bag. "Not just the food. That bag. May I?"

"Oh, sure!" Ella said with an irritation that Dime hoped wasn't too serious. Ella rummaged through the bag, moving the balms, bandages, and a few tools into pouches on her tunic.

They didn't speak as Dime hobbled back toward the burrows, trying not to go too fast on her untested ankle. The common area was calm as they approached, but then several screeches sounded. Juni was not among the gathered newts, nor was Stern Eyes, Dime noticed.

"How do you say her name?" Dime whispered to Ella. "Stern Eyes. I want to say it right."

"You won't!" Ella said with a snort. "Don't try! Just say this." Ella made a soothing sound. "It's respectful. Now don't vary it or that meaning will change."

Dime tried not to think about that as Stern Eyes emerged from the closest burrow, humming in a low tone and with a face even more stern than normal. Dime headed right toward her, making the best and most respectful cooing sound she could muster. With another thought, she pulled every pouch of size off of her jacket and laid it next to Ella's large bag, filled with the food she'd brought for their journey back.

Stern Eyes rose up and bellowed at full volume as the other newts ran back toward their burrows. Unflinching, yet unsure how to react, Dime just stood there, hoping it would not be seen as defiance. Yet, she could detect the unmistakable expression of satisfaction. Stern Eyes waited, not touching the contents of the bag. "Let's go," Ella whispered. "You did fine."

Without another word, Dime and Ella turned and retraced their steps, headed toward a place that Dime hoped could not be stranger than the last.

As she left, a weight of sorrow set in at the thought that perhaps she would not see Juni for a very long time. In the distance, Dime heard a howl, one that reminded her of a ch'pyr, calling for family.

If Ella noticed Dime's tears, she did not mention them.

Interlude

Lunn was running out of fuel for his lamps. His hands unsteady, he tapped the metal base against the carved table, hoping he could run this one for at least a few more bells.

Once retired, he'd moved here to a small home on the mountainside of Nor Lodon. And one by one, the pyrsi he'd loved most had died. He still had grandchildren in the city, and he supposed they had families, but they'd stopped visiting long ago.

The only visitor now was the transport, bringing him food, supplies, and his publications. Sometimes an Inspector came to check on his health, but it was fine. It was always fine, and he was glad when they left.

Lunn spent all his time now poring through his publications, one after the other. Stacks of publications, that had told the truth, he now knew.

They'd been right about the fairies. He'd seen the last *Caller*. Fairies. Fairies in Lodon. They'd said it was lies. It wasn't lies. The beasts had flown into the city, used their valence to wound and destroy. This was just the start.

The *Caller* didn't say those things. But the *Caller* was controlled by the Circles. Spreading lies was all the Circles had ever done.

These pyrsi. They got it. If they were right about the fairies, they were right about other things too. Lunn tried to calm himself. He was too scared to go out now; his windows were covered with every spare blanket he owned, and only the lamplight flickered in his large front room. He missed watching the curved rows of towers below and the birds that circled the mountain slope, but he could not risk the fairies finding him here.

The Great War was returning. Lunn knew this. They never said it directly in the publications; the Circles would never let them. But Lunn understood their clever words. He knew what they meant. And he agreed. The Great War would come again, and the return of the fairies had proven it.

If the Violence had returned, he would not succumb to it. He was a good ma'pyr and kept right with Sol. But, still, he could help.

He grasped the pen, his aged fingers now almost the color of the ink itself. Holding his pen hand as steady as he could with the other, Lunn scrawled the transport stop onto the envelope, the one in the publication. He slid the paynote inside and set it next to the donation he'd already sealed for the freeshops.

From within his darkened home, he huddled by the lamplight, hoping that when the fairies returned, they would leave him alone.

Act 3

THE BEGINNING

"My spouse was a Fo-ror," Ella noted as they worked their way up another hill.

Dime almost tripped over her stick. Ella had seemed absorbed in thought, and the hike was long, slow, and exhausting, so they had walked thus far without conversation. She assumed at some point they'd stop and rest, and there would be time for questions then. In truth, Dime was over being surprised by anything. But this was something. *Married to a fairy!*

"Some Circles agent found out, investigating reports made by some ch'pyrsi exploring the old woods. Or, the 'dark woods' as you've probably heard them. We live out that way, or, I do now, in a small tower. With Friend."

But Dime had spent cycles in the IC. It wouldn't make sense that she hadn't—

"You're probably thinking you would have heard if it were true. Yet, as I'm sure you know, there are secrets and then there are secrets. The report went straight to the Light himself. Not Sala, as this was a while back, before she was chosen.

"He visited us on his own, like actually showed up at our home, demanding that Suzanne must leave." Ella wheezed. "Ha, you try telling Suzanne what to do—even if you *are* the Light. Or, especially if you're the Light!" For a moment, a spark lit Ella's eyes, fading as soon as it appeared.

"Once he saw she was going to be stubborn about it, it was more important to him that no one learned of us than it was to try and oust us. So he spread stories of a dark witch on the edge of the woods. Made it a crime to approach, for pyrsi's own protection. I'm sure the record was 'sealed' or 'burned' or whatever you pyrsi do with facts that you don't accept." She sneered.

You pyrsi? Dime's instinct was to defend that, but she was feeling uncertain herself, and Ella wasn't pausing for her input.

"And thus the witch of the woods was born. Came from some ridiculous old story about a fe'pyr that hexed visitors. No, he wouldn't say she had valence, because Suzanne did have valence, and used it quite effectively, and that would just be a little too close to the truth. And, since I'd come into the city sometimes for supplies and he knew it, he spread my description as this witch. I could hardly buy fruit in the market after that.

"It's faded over time, but the story gets passed down by those with an itch for superstition and not enough else to do. Suzanne, to your precious Light, didn't even exist. Sala, if she even knows the story, probably thinks she's still there."

Dime was taken aback by the bitter edge to Ella's tone and almost advised her to leave Dime out of her assumptions. But, she didn't know this fe'pyr at all. She'd become so accustomed to odd events over these past few turns, she'd taken it at face value that a random fe'pyr would show up in the middle of a newt colony to walk her home. Even now, Dime followed Ella along without question. For all she knew, Ella was leading her to the fairies.

Except, Dime knew she wasn't. Dime had always had a sense of when pyrsi were or weren't telling the truth. She didn't know what Ella's angle on all this was yet, but Dime trusted everything she said. Even the idea of a Ja-lal being married to a Fo-ror. Which she couldn't imagine. But now believed.

Still, the attitude. For now, her breaths short and everything swirling in her mind, she let the comments slide.

Using the beach stick to walk was slow, painful, and wearisome, though she found the travel easier as the sand gave way to firmer soil, scruffy grasses, and tall, waving stalks that helped block the wind. Ella stopped and waited when Dime paused at a cluster of spiky orange flowers to breathe in their sharp fragrance. "Aren't they nice?" Ella commented.

They never stopped for long. As the bells passed and the terrain began to dry out again, Dime realized they must be close to Sol's Reach. Also, that they would not be passing through the forest this way. She supposed they must be skirting its wesside edge. She wondered how far they were from the cliff.

"Will we, uh, have to scale the cliff?" Dime considered that, despite her injuries, they didn't have climbing equipment. She had no idea how they'd manage.

"You cross at its ends. The wesside dwindles down to the shore; it's passable on foot for one narrow stretch."

Passable! As in, pyrsi could just wander down to the land of the fairies? That didn't show up on IC maps.

At least relieved of any worries of cliff climbing, she plodded along, trying to keep her mind off all her pains and soreness and just get herself home. As she sorted through the information in her mind, concern focused again on her family. Before they got back into Sol's Reach, Dime needed to decide her next move.

She couldn't be seen in Lodon, but it would also be the best place to gather facts and news. And she had no idea what had transpired in the city these past turns.

Ella must know more than they'd discussed; it seemed she'd been out looking for Dime. So, she probably knew of the invasion. At least Ella wouldn't need to be convinced of the presence of fairies in the city.

"So you knew the fairies came for me—I suppose?" Dime

felt a little ch'pyrish between the simple words and their relative tardiness.

"The rumors are all over. Even Sala can't quash them. Stories across the city of flying fairies. Big shiny wings. Capes and hoods like criminals. Some insist they knocked over walls or burned down portions of the market, despite there being no such damage or witnesses. Of course, they say that was the Maintenance Circle performing a speedy cleanup."

"A wall was broken, though I don't think on purpose. I didn't notice any fires." Dime tried to recall what she'd seen as she ran through the streets.

"Stories are generally muddled when told by a crowd," Ella offered. "Though I put no amount of cover-up past your Circles, or past the Seats for that matter. Either way, I saw no signs of damage myself. No signs of Fo-ror. From all reports, they chased you out and haven't reappeared since. I still have a few good sources in the city, and they told me that you were the one involved. High-level Intel Circle agent said to have just left. You can imagine the rumors that in itself would cause.

"Now, I don't know a thing about this Fe'Diamond, other than her curiously fairy-sympathetic name and her counter-intuitive career choices. But, as I've already explained to you, I have an interest in such things. So I gathered some emergency supplies and set out to see what I could find about the missing agent.

"My first stop was to visit my beach-dwelling friends, as they are excellent trackers, don't mind giving a pyr a ride, and are well-willing to break into the Heartland if I find them a way in. I had no chance to ask them a thing; there you were, a sad-looking nudie plopped down on the edge of the Beds. 'Alright, who's this?' I thought. And then the newts told me what they believed, and it was nothing like what I expected to hear. So it seems we may have a situation."

The Beds? The newts? Information about me? A slew of new questions began to formulate in Dime's mind. But Ella spoke again.

"Now, on that subject, I've told you a fair bit about myself, but I have no idea who you are."

Dime recognized the technique: a clear change in subject. But Ella was right; Dime hadn't told her much of anything. It had felt as though Ella already knew her. Or must have. The older fe'pyr had traveled all the way across the cliff to find her, after all. Dime struggled, trying to figure what to say.

"I'm Fe'Dime. I'm twenty cycles old and moving toward twenty-one." Now she really felt like a lower-grade student. "I worked for the Intel Circle, and the day I left, I was pursued by three Fo-ror—completely out of nowhere—who attempted to *capture* me with strange ropes. I didn't know why. I still don't know why. I'm not sure I actually believed they existed.

"They started pushing stuff around, so I tried to draw them away from Lodon and at the same time lose them so I could regroup and develop a plan. Instead, I drove all the way to the end of Sol's Reach in some sort of wild fury, fell over the cliff, and survived long enough for Juni to find me. Now you've found me also.

"I'm starting to feel like I'm going to make it through all this, at least for today, but I'm worried about my family. Mostly that they might be worried about me. I have a father, a spouse, and two children in the city. I've got to get to them."

Dime whipped her head around and she stopped in place. "You have sources. Were there any captures? Charges? Injuries? Anything related to my family? Or that could impact them?"

Ella paused. "As of when I left, I'd heard nothing. They're probably lying low. I'm not certain that Sala or her agents would seek them out right away. Sometimes when asking questions risks turning an unpleasant story into an unpleasant fact, our leaders prefer not to ask. So your family may be fine for now. I hope they are."

Dime appreciated the sincerity in Ella's voice, and she felt a growing connection with the unordinary fe'pyr. "I'd thought about hiding somewhere in the outlands and getting word to the fairies so they wouldn't go back to the city. But if they think I'm dead, maybe I'm safe to go back. And I mean, how would I get them word anyway without telling everyone in Sol's Reach?" Dime sighed, frustrated and wishing she knew more.

She started walking forward again, remembering they were trying to keep moving. "I've got to go back to Lodon," she said. "Don't you agree?"

Ella took a long time to answer, as they walked along side by side. "I think, if you are careful, you can stay out of sight, and then we can plan." She blinked. "Sorry . . . *we* . . . it's just that I . . . I think I can help. It would be . . . more interesting . . . than sitting around the tower."

Dime wasn't sure where to begin. She wasn't sure why Ella would want to help her, but if she needed the one pyr who had a connection to the fairies, she'd found her. And it wasn't really a coincidence, not if everyone knew what had happened. Dime was still grappling with that herself. As many times as she casually referenced fairies popping into her living room, it still didn't seem possible. Fairies, after all.

"Ella?"

Ella returned the inquiry with a side glance.

"You said your spouse *was* a Fo-ror. Has she . . . joined memory?" Dime thought she knew the answer, but it would be a dreadful thing to misunderstand.

Ella's face tightened and her words became terse. "Yes. Many cycles now. Fe'Suzannelina of the village of Noruh. An outer village, out sur toward Home Sha. She was a botanist, chef, healer, poet— She was everything this world needed. She was my best friend."

"I'm sorry." Dime glanced again at Ella's skin, dark enough to exceed Dime's own age but not dark enough that it was normal to lose a spouse, and not cycles ago. So much had been taken from her. Her city. Her identity. Her spouse. And, she had not mentioned children or a current relationship, just someone or something she called Friend. It didn't sound like the way one would refer to a homemate, so then, perhaps Ella lived alone, outcast for a reason no longer even valid. Or maybe, that was never valid.

But then, without her spouse, Ella could go back to Lodon. Yet she hadn't. Not in all these cycles. Dime was curious about the reasons why, and almost as if Ella had read her mind, she changed the subject again with a decided glare.

"We're almost out of the Heartland now, or the fringe of it where we were. The Crossing is ahead. Assuming you haven't been there, it's a funny place."

"Like, funny, ha ha?"

"What?" Ella grimaced. "No, like odd." She paused. "It was funny one time, with a Fo-ror trader who had a bird companion." Ella's expression softened.

Dime almost asked, but there was another question on her mind and she didn't want to lose it. "Is *the Heartland*—is it *the Undergrowth*?" This was getting ridiculous. And embarrassing. Dime had spent a career in Intel yet appeared to know so little. Or at least her knowledge ended at the cliff. As she had been told it must be.

"Oh, sure. Of course. It's what the Fo-ror call their lands. Just as the Ja-lal call theirs Sol's Reach."

"What do the Fo-ror call Sol's Reach?"

"What?"

"If we each have our own names for things, do they have their own for Sol's Reach?"

"Oh, that. Yes. The Barrens."

"They call Sol's Reach the *Barrens*?" Dime remembered the lush green canopy of the edge of the Undergrowth and almost conceded the point. But, no. As beautiful as the forest was, Sol's Reach was anything but barren.

"The Crossing is a funny place," Ella continued, "because it isn't supposed to exist."

Dime thought about this for a stride. She'd been taught that since the Great War, the Ja-lal and Fo-ror had gone off to exist in separate worlds, thankfully divided by a non-navigable cliff, lest their unsalvageable relationship ever again bring the Violence. But then, why was there a *crossing*? Images sprung to mind of a big sign—Welcome to Sol's Reach—and a tourist shop selling carved desk baubles. It probably wasn't that.

"And, like any place that doesn't exist, there's no protection for those daring to visit it. Such places are usually either inherently safe or inherently dangerous, depending on who ends up in charge."

"Let me guess," Dime said. "This one falls under dangerous. But— Certainly—" She couldn't finish that sentence.

"The Violence? Oh, not like that. Tickling its borders— Swindling? Contraband? Quite a bit. I would say, though, that there would be social repercussions for being seen in a place like that, so it keeps law-abiding pyrsi from seeking out whether it really exists."

"But," Dime thought aloud, "anyone who sees you there is also there." She'd used the line often when her children were embarrassed to go to an uncool shop.

Ella shrugged. "It's complicated. Ill-meaning pyrsi may enlist confused youth to act on their behalf. Or one can refer to some 'report' that you were there, rather than admit they saw you firsthand. Yet that's rare; there's no one going to or through the Crossing who has any incentive to talk about it.

"And remember, none of that matters anyway. If the Circles choose to make your life difficult, they can do so without revealing the real reason why."

That's true. Dime was getting annoyed at herself for continuing to act so naïve—she resolved to stop doing it. The last few turns had just been so odd; Dime needed to pull her banners back together.

"Your precious Circles are not the heroes they claim to be." Ella grunted.

Now, this is enough.

"Hey. I quit, remember." Dime felt a little satisfaction saying it.

"So you quit," Ella snapped. "Did you change anything?"

That was really too far. Dime was tired of this insinuation that by leaving, she was giving up, especially from some stranger. She had been pounding her figurative fists against the gnarled door of reason for as long as she'd been in any position to do so, and she was tired of hearing that *she* was somehow the problem, and not the others who promoted traditions they knew fostered inequity and even danger. You know, maybe she was as mad as the fe'pyr beside her. Maybe she should be.

"Did you?" Dime retorted.

"So that does make The Crossing more dangerous," Ella continued on as if not hearing her, "in the sense that untrustworthy behaviors sometimes pass without consequence."

The diversion was so obvious, Dime couldn't even stay annoyed.

"And your case is . . . unique. Until we know who is interested in you, we'll need to keep your identity concealed. I hate having to go through the place at all," Ella gestured to Dime's leg, "but you're in no shape to swim or scale cliffs—"

"And I gave our food away," Dime added.

"See, and I was trying to be polite. Anyway, won't be the first risky thing I've done." Ella nodded at Dime. "Nor you."

The Crossing. A place where Fo-ror and Ja-lal apparently, what, visit? Dime felt frustrated by each new revelation, as if she hadn't been a senior Intel official. Yet, for all her knowledge and insight and cycles of studying, she was now in a world strictly out of bounds to her and her pyrsi. Except, not? *Ugh.*

She wished Ador were here; she would have a lot to ask him. She felt a pang, remembering she was a real pyr with real friends. She missed Ador.

More, she missed Dayn. She imagined the warmth of holding each other's arms again, the feel of their cheeks, brushing.

Dayn must be worried, but she knew Ador would be there for him. One comforting thought.

They rested twice, though briefly; without food and with almost no water left, they needed to press. At each stop, Ella reset Dime's bandage on her arm with clean cloth and fresh balm. "I've always been slow to heal," Dime said, feeling bad that her injuries continued to slow their progress. "Everyone's had advice for me on it, that it's my diet or my rest or my hobbies. Gets old."

"It's none of those," Ella murmured, but when Dime tried to ask her more, Ella gathered their belongings and started out again, leaving Dime grumbling and scrambling to catch up.

Her ankle ached, and Dime worried that she'd already pushed it too far, but Ella hastened her steps now, her eyes focused ahead on reaching this Crossing, to return to Sol's Reach. Dime grew increasingly certain that Ella was hiding something from her. Before this was over, Dime would find out. For now, though, she accepted the need to stay focused on their first goal: the Crossing.

"Is that it?" Dime asked, as a low cliff came into view. It was nothing like the towering force of nature she'd imagined and had apparently tumbled over, just a low cliff with a pass worn through it. More like a hill. *The Great Hill*, she joked to herself.

She stared up at the ridge ahead. It would still be a long journey to Lodon, but the idea that home, any part of home, was past that ridge brought her a wave of comfort. She refused a few tears that tried to form. First she had to make it through this place, whose risk to her she was certain Ella understated.

There were no signs or boutiques, but a path started to form, leading toward the pass. Dime's breathing grew heavy as the path turned steeply uphill. Ella stopped and pulled a few items out of her bulging side pouches. First, she handed Dime a *hood*. Dime gasped, and involuntarily shook her head. Meanwhile, Ella wrapped her scarf over and around her own.

"No righteous Circles talk here. This is a different place, outside their control. Here, you mind your own business."

"We'll *have* to draw suspicion with these."

"Sure!" Ella said, her voice tinged with sarcasm. "Let's not draw suspicion! If you want, you can just stroll through on your wounded leg with your big, viney tats and hope your assailants didn't leave a scout, just in case you survived Dime's Big Adventure."

Hmpf. "Point taken." Yet, she was not prepared when Ella reached forward with an art stick and started sketching on her forehead. It didn't take long to surmise that Ella was giving her a large hemsa, to peek out from the front of her hood. It would be revealed as surface ink upon inspection, but maybe from a distance it would do. "Do I at least get to know which one?"

"Maybe better that you don't," Ella said with a chuckle. "But I have simply noted that you are most definitely not in favor of the Light." She paused. "I thought about adding volume under your cloak, to imply you were Fo-ror. A Ja-lal and Fo-ror traveling together would be least likely to be approached for fear of any association. But your tattoos—" Ella traced the air over the vines reaching out onto Dime's face. "They mark you. As they mark me also. I can't just scribble them all over."

Dime had been so distracted by the fairies' hair she had not fully considered that they did not wear tattoos. *It must be so hard to describe pyrsi there.*

"So, a couple of suspicious Ja-lal we will be," Ella finished.

Dime laughed. Ella looked away.

"Still," Ella said, "keep your head low, don't draw attention, and let me do the talking. Oh, and do you have any notes? There have to be paynotes in that jacket. Never met anyone with the Circles that didn't carry a wad."

"Just signed," Dime said, letting the remark pass as she slipped on the hood. "I used all my unsigned notes to get away." Dime tended to sign her paynotes, preferring security to anonymity.

"Pfffft. We can't have that," Ella said. "It's fine. I have enough. Buy me a ferm sometime. Or clean the drains on my tower. I do *not* like getting on that ladder. Suzanne," she grumbled, shaking a hand toward Sol.

Dime chuckled but not for long as they trudged up the final hill, quite a lot steeper than the previous one. "Anyone sell toothcars here? We could use a ride."

"They do," Ella said. "Which apparently I need to buy. And no more talking; your accent is a trail mix of low and high class. It would be a signature for anyone searching for you."

Dime had a lot of comments to that, but she pressed her mouth shut. Ahead, the path opened into what looked like a basin. The rocks rose stiffly to eas and wes, framed by large piles of boulders. A few were roughly carved in spirit-like shapes, though Dime wasn't sure if it was art or just someone with extra time.

Within the basin, an oversize toothcar was hooked to a wide cart filled with crates. Several tents were spread across the area, their openings flapping in a dusty wind that caused Dime to raise a sleeve over her mouth. Crates, sheds, and machines sat in the distance, and burnt oil fumes wafted by.

There were fairies here, as well as Ja-lal. "Would the fairies take our paynotes?" she whispered. "Theirs must be different." Dime could not take her eyes from a fairy's flapping set of wings in the distance.

"Oh, it's all different. The Fo-ror don't have currency. Paynotes are dishonorable. Provisions are allocated based on 'need.' A Fo-ror is best respected when xe gives to others, and I mean, isn't that nice. Yet, honor has its loopholes. Currency is forbidden, but barter is just two pyrsi giving gifts. Also, it's hard to track.

"We'll want to find a Ja-lal. Looking as we do, the Fo-ror won't approach us here anyway. Unless we approach them. Which, at this moment, I don't intend to do. Now, quiet, please. They'll be listening."

Dime found the haphazard layout of the Crossing unsettling; it was comprised mostly of battered tents that looked like they could be whisked away on short notice. There were only a few partially permanent structures, and those bore no windows, just thin notches to let in light or allow a pyr to peer outward. Everything felt uncertain, out of place. Nothing looked arranged, or even built out from the basin's center. Everything looked as if it'd just been set down there for a moment.

And fairies. Walking around, even flying. Their big, iridescent wings were as awestriking as she remembered. No, more so—they were colors and art and motion. Each muscular body flew with such ease, tassels and locks of hair swaying behind them.

She shouldn't be here. They needed to go. Dime wished they could just keep their heads down and zip on through. But she was so hungry now she could barely stand it, her leg was so sore she could barely walk, and it wouldn't be much longer until night fell again.

Once they crossed through, they could stop in a village for supplies, but it was clear Ella felt safer in this place-that-did-not-exist than one of the outlying villages. Besides, Dime was not as familiar with the wesside of the plains, so they'd have to search for a town.

The plains. At least she was back to Sol's Reach. Just a few steps away.

Her heart ached for her home.

Trying not to cough from the dust blowing through the basin, Dime kept her head low as they walked through. Despite being a place where pyrsi didn't want to be noticed, they sure made it a certainty to notice others. Dime could feel every gaze, every assessment from within the tents and block structures as she walked past. Hidden eyes, all affixed to her.

"Looking for food, not trouble," Ella called, in a voice unlike her own. "Also a car for two. Unsigned paynotes; not forged. Tips for brevity." A pyr's bare gray arm waved from a tent flap next to a low block wall. "Don't move," Ella warned Dime. "And above all, keep your necklace hidden. *Holy Sol.*" Ella muttered something else as she walked toward the patched tent.

Fighting the urge to reach for it, Dime felt her pendant, where she normally kept it, nestled under her shirt. Ella was already a small figure in the distance. She felt self-conscious standing in the wind with her hood and cloak blowing around her. Yet, with whatever fake hemsa Ella had given her, she realized she shouldn't be so self-conscious. Angry, perhaps. Defiant. *What would an outlaw do here? An outlaw that had been ordered to wait, anyway.*

She set her stance and turned slowly, as though she were looking to see who was there, as if she could see into each structure through its canvas, blocks, or boards. Several pyrsi looked away or closed the flaps of their tents. Above, a dark shape came into view, and the fairy—or Fo-ror she supposed she should say—landed near her with a small cloud of dust. Dime tensed but tried not to show any surprise.

"Gift for the bladetrader," xe called. Ignoring Dime, the fairy walked over to the steps of a large building. Another pyr, without wings, opened the door and they both disappeared behind it.

Other than the transacting of business, it was quiet. Pyrsi sat. And stared. Or hid behind their walls. Dime was relieved as a take passed and no one approached her. If this was the one crossing between the lands, it would seem her pursuers would monitor it for her return.

Except, then, the fairies may indeed think she was dead. As Ella said, she needed to get home and stay out of view. Once someone recognized her, she couldn't be sure word wouldn't spread to the fairies. Now that she knew there was a whole *town* of mingling and news. Her head almost shook in disbelief, but she held still.

There were options to consider—once she got out of here. She wasn't going to live her life in hiding; that was for sure.

Dime was starting to feel she wasn't exuding much toughness standing in the path, and she worried about drawing attention. She doubted pyrsi loitered in the streets here. Pulling her utility knife from her jacket, she turned it in the air—not quite flipping it, but rolling it in her fingers pretty well, she thought with pride. It was a habit she had picked up during bored turns in the field, but, hey, maybe it looked like a criminal thing to do.

"Put that away!" Ella hissed, hustling toward her on the path. "We need to go now. I have what we need, but I dodged a few of their questions and they know it, so we can't risk any more contact. Now, over here."

Behind a wall, Ella led her to a dual-pedal toothcar with a huge dent in the roof, tossing a large bag into the back bin. Dime slid her walking stick into the back of the rough-looking car, which reeked of cheap gear grease. "How *old* is this?"

"You wanna go buy one? With your signed note? Maybe hire us a couple of pedalers while you're at it?"

"Ok, ok, I'm sorry," Dime conceded. "But I can't wait to take this hood off; it feels so *shady*."

"It is shady. And not until we're out of sight. Now, rest your bad ankle there. You half-pedal with the other foot, I'll pedal with these beauties, and we'll make it work. Also, yes, this is a piece of junk. And I despise driving."

Dime laughed to herself as she did her best to pedal with one foot. The laughter turned quickly to pained grumbling, as it turned out that one-foot pedaling was much more difficult than two. Instead of relying on the motion of the gears, Dime had to constantly raise and lower her foot, kicking the narrow footrest rather than pedaling it.

The imbalanced teeth clanked and ground against the dry rocks as Ella switched the gears, and they cranked away from the Crossing. "Here," Ella said, handing her a bunch of longfruit and a hunk of stale bread, which Dime chomped into immediately. "Not too fast," she warned. "You haven't eaten anything proper in turns; your gut will punish you for rushing."

"I'm naw a ba'pyr," Dime mumbled through a bite of bread.

They waited until it was dark to stop and take another rest. Exhausted and now with both feet sore, Dime ate her meal cold, found a flat enough patch of ground, and fell right to sleep.

As they pedaled on across the open plains, Dime was glad for the darkness. With the shapes of plateaus and gullies around them, she hoped one small toothcar would be hard to spot from a distance.

She couldn't shake the image of bands of fairies sweeping the land, closing in and tying her with ropes. Unless they could see in the dark. She had heard of that with some animals; the newts clearly could.

"Ella, can they see in the dark?"

"What? Who? What are you going on about? Oh, Fo-ror." Ella grunted. "They see as well as you do, which is better than me. But no, if you mean as well as the newts, not like that. The newts' vision is exceptional, day or night."

Between the old car, their tired state, and Dime's injuries, they moved along slowly. She'd pedaled all the way to the cliff from Lodon almost in a trance, but now, she felt every bump and muscle ache.

While Dime hadn't seen any signs of the fairies or any active pursuit, Ella didn't want to risk more exposure than needed. Dime agreed. And so, while slow, they kept as steady a pace as they could, resting frequently but not for long each time. It was a measure faster than walking, Dime reminded herself. And it was a nice night, with clear skies and gentle breezes.

"I don't sleep much at night," Dime mentioned, making conversation as they rode between a series of plateaus. "I find night peaceful and I prefer to enjoy it. My Circlemates joked that I was lazy, but no one worked harder than me during the day, so I tried not to worry about it. Sorry," she added, looking at Ella. "I'm saying random things."

"The Fo-ror see night this way," Ella said with some hesitation. "They catch up on their work during the daylight hours, then enjoy their families and friends or their own hobbies at night, as it can be deeply dark in the depths of the forest, where the trees shield the nightlight.

"Their schedules are more patterned around each other, not as free-form as you're used to in Lodon. The Ja-lal, with the open nightlight and a lamp in every room, design their schedules with less regard to night and day. Or to each other."

"It's true," Dime agreed. "I have friends that sleep every several bells, and others who go long stretches without rest then long stretches with. Depends what you do, of course. And what appointments you keep. I sleep regularly enough, but I reserve things I like to do for when it's dark."

Ella did not object when, while they rested by a small pond, Dime scrubbed the artificial hemsa from her forehead. It could only cause alarm in Sol's Reach, and without the hood, her other markings would identify her to anyone looking.

As they traveled, ate, and rested in pattern, Dime recognized the landscape. With the expanses of the beaches and grassy hills well behind them, the plains and plateaus of her homeland were rocky and dry. Clear roads now separated large elevations of rock, and Dime could see lamps shining from villages in the background.

"This old car will draw attention," Ella said as the lights of one village drew closer. "They'll think we time-traveled. Let's sell it and walk the last stretch to Lodon."

Dime waited in the shadows, her hood now packed into Ella's pouch, as a pyr came out and inspected the vehicle. Papers changed hands, and Ella hurried away.

"Sold it for a tenth of what I paid for it, but such is business at the Crossing," Ella grumbled. "At least you owe me a ferm over it. Just glad he took it, really; the whole pile of junk reeked of disreputation. Also, I didn't want him to start to remember where he had heard of my tattoos." Ella paused. "And, sorry, you were right. What a poop car. I couldn't stand it another stride."

Sol was rising again as they approached Lodon on foot. Dime still used her walking stick, though the soreness was much less pronounced after her foot's extended rest. The other foot, though, was now tired and angry from pedaling so far. Dime had never appreciated the act of walking so much. She felt a new understanding for Tum's routine.

Family in mind, her heart pounded as they made their way over the next hill and the Great Gates of Lodon formed in her view, the stone towers beyond rising up against their hazy mountain backdrop. Sol's first light burst from behind, casting long shadows like a hand, reaching to welcome them. She'd spent her life in this city, and the fact that it was still here, still something familiar, reawakened her.

She hastened her wobbly steps, thinking of Dayn, and Luja, and Tum. Of Da-da. She would see them soon.

"Stop," Ella called out, throwing a hand in caution. "What's this?"

The main gates of Lodon loomed large, but rather than a dotting of fare-takers and leisure strollers, there was an organized line of pyrsi, wearing bright colors and carrying large banners atop thick poles. Pyrsi entering the city walked between them, like a greeting line at a reception, except some stopped and bowed, while others hurried.

It was like she had returned to a different place after all. Dime had no idea what this could mean. Were they guarding the city, now?

Ella pulled a small glass from her jacket, expanding its concentric metal rings to peer ahead. "Well, this is a twist. Sol's Pillars! Seems you've wrested the slime from the muck."

Sol's Pillars—a fringe political group. Dime knew all about them; the IC kept a running list of their activity and suspected registration, making sure nothing got out of hand. They did this with any organization speaking independently of the Circles, including Ador's group, the Free Winds. Speech itself wasn't a crime—and Sol forbid it ever would be—but in reality it was punished with equal fervor and less attention.

The Circles didn't like the Free Winds, and they used their network to keep its leadership out of positions of power or influence. But that's where the comparison ended. While the Free Winds challenged the laws set by the Circles, and sometimes the structure and authority of the Circles themselves, Sol's Pillars heralded their exclusionary views in loud rallies, calling for a re-strengthening of prosperity.

Prosperity, they said, was central to the continued survival of the Ja-lal. Pyrsi must be encouraged to thrive, free from lowered standards and the threat of criminals. Society must be strengthened, not weakened, to survive.

Perhaps without context, Dime would have agreed. Prosperity *was* essential to taking care of all pyrsi. But Dime herself had sweat and clawed her way up to the role that she wanted as part of a low-class family, a child to a maintenance worker who'd found her lying in a sky alley.

And so, as a pyr who had always been seen as low-class first, she understood that the undertone of these dreams of success was a sense of social boundaries—who deserved this freedom, who was safe to include, and who would have to earn the right even to try.

A new reality struck her as she watched the pyrsi below, raising and lowering their banners. Sol's Pillars frequently used the fairies' lurking threat as a rallying cry for their supporters, the reason the Ja-lal must stay focused and sharp. Some viewed the reference as a metaphor against immorality, but Dime now considered their messages in a new light. Speeches of renewed prosperity, references to Ja-lal as the pyrsi of Sol, hints at the unfairness of the fairies stealing and hoarding, of the need for permanent peace—

While she found their words divisive and loathsome, she had not considered their full implication. To Dime, the fairies had been distant, fictional. To Sol's Pillars, they were a match, ready to be lit.

Dime understood, as she was sure Ella did beside her, that their presence here, in the open and wearing their sigils, was no coincidence. The rumors of the winged invaders must have been spread, and believed, and in pyrsi's fear, they turned to the organization they most trusted to protect them. Sol's Pillars had been viewed as a fringe group, warning against a symbolic enemy. Now, they had been validated.

"Sala must be beside herself," Dime muttered. Ella, who looked as shocked to see the amassed crowds as Dime was, said nothing. Her gaze hardened.

"Can't risk it. You must know that." Ella motioned to Dime. "Now, with me. We're too close already. They'll be at all the entrances, I'm sure. They may be watching for Fo-ror, but they don't know what happened at the cliff. From their perspective, you left with the fairies. Every one of them probably has a sketch of you on hand. I'm sure you're all over the *Caller*, your name and description."

"Who cares?" Dime glared in fury at the lines of pyrsi. "It's my home; I'm welcome in it. What could anyone do to me? I have no career to lose!"

"Dime," Ella whispered. "There is more to this than you know. I don't understand it myself, but we need to talk. Please. Let's talk. And . . . not here."

"But my family! If I'm in the *Caller*, or even the street reports, they'll be scared. I'm not going to let these—"

"Dime. I have contacts in the city and information that they'll want. I'll find a way to check on anyone you name. I didn't know how things had escalated here; you're not healed. At worst, we'll need to run and we can't. At best, they'll spread news of your injuries as propaganda that the Fo-ror have returned the Violence and so it can no longer be stayed. Please—we're not ready for this. We need to go."

Dime started to think through her options. She had snuck out; she could sneak in.

Ella got right in her face. "Do you trust me or not?"

"I don't even know you!" Dime felt rude snapping back; the fe'pyr may have saved her life, and she'd grown attached to her during their long, difficult journey. But Dime would make her own decisions and Ella was stepping too far.

"That's not what I asked."

Ok. There was something Ella wasn't telling her and wasn't going to tell her here. Dime knew there was no danger greater than a lack of information. *Harm and destruction.* "Fine, we'll go." Dime remembered that Ella lived by the dark woods. She tried not to think about another endless stretch of walking. Still fueled by anger at what she had just seen, Dime was almost feeling tough about it.

Taking in a long view of the walled city and pretending Dayn could hear her thoughts, Dime turned to her left and hobbled off behind Ella down a long, shrubby hill.

Now without their car and with Ella insisting that no one else must see them, they continued on, ducking across roads and walking in the shelter of rocks or hills when possible. Frequently, Ella gritted her teeth and muttered to herself. Dime tried to ignore her and instead sort this new information. Dime had always thrived on information; it was an agent's blood.

The Fo-ror wanted her for some reason she couldn't imagine. Now, Sol's Pillars could be looking for her too. They wouldn't try to capture her, at least she hoped it hadn't gone so far, but she knew Ella was right that Sol's Pillars wouldn't hesitate to use her for propaganda against the Fo-ror. But, it wasn't like she was on the fairies' side either. They *did* try to capture her. Maybe she should go into Lodon and warn the others, dealing with Sol's Pillars as best she could.

No. She was not going to deal with them, whatever that meant. Dime was finished placating ignorance for the sake of calm. She saw now the direction they pointed, to hostility, to—she forced herself to think it—even to a rekindling of the Great War.

Dime would not risk helping them pave a path to the Violence. She would not associate with those who fostered superiority. Also, they were creepy and Dime had standards. She'd avoid them until she knew more, at the least.

Ador. She could send a message to Ador, to enlist his help. Though he'd been held back from traditional power in Lodon, he was connected in his own ways. She knew never to underestimate him. He could sneak her into town, keep her hidden, and help her figure out what was going on. She turned back over her shoulder, seeing only a silhouette of the tall towers against the clouds.

Frustrated that she was leaving the problem right when she arrived to resolve it, Dime began to mutter as much as Ella. After a while, they were two grumpy fe'pyrsi, lugging big bags up and down the steepening hills.

"Here. One more meal." Ella stopped and exhaled. "If you agree."

"*Hmpf,*" Dime wasn't sure they should stop now, but she was hungry and kind of mad. She eyed Ella, trying to decide her position.

"I'm tired of dragging this food and I don't see to waste it," Ella added. "I have supplies at home, so we might as well stop for a bit. It's not much of a biscuit, but it'll do."

Dime looked over the hill, realizing why Ella had chosen to stop here. They'd see anyone approaching from Lodon before they were seen; they had time to move along.

"But no fire," Ella said.

Of course no fire.

The food they had bought at the Crossing was plain and not fresh, and Dime, especially in light of her recent hardships, couldn't shake the craving for a hot patty melt with pan-fried chips. What she settled for was another bunch of longfruit, a stack of crackers, and what was left of a preserved garlic spread.

The garlic spread did help. "Never met a garlic I didn't like," Dime said with a grin.

"Suzanne was the same." Ella's face turned again. "I'm sorry, I don't mean to bring her up so often. But, with the Fo-ror, and . . . other things. It brings back memories."

Dime's spirit sunk at the heartbreak in Ella's eyes, undulled by the passing of the cycles. "May I ask you? How did you meet a Fo-ror in the first place?"

Ella stared her down for a long stride, and Dime almost took the question back. Then Ella answered.

"I was a journalist. Still am, though that's between us. Back then I was always looking for the next piece, the big edge, the story that would make pyrsi flock to the theaters to hear it. The story to lead the *Caller*. So I went after the biggest one I could imagine."

"The Fo-ror?" Dime asked, leaning forward.

"No. The newts." Ella took a sip of cold tea. "I moved in with them, basically, approaching a little each turn until they began to trust me. I learned to communicate with them. I understood their culture. I had the best story of my career, built over long seasons away, hidden in a place I was never supposed to go. It was a masterpiece."

The wind whistled by over the hill.

"Well, don't you want to know what happened?"

"Oh," Dime said. "I figured you were going to tell me. Um, what happened?"

Ella cleared her throat. "I didn't submit it."

"Ok." Dime wasn't sure where this was going.

"It was wrong. They trusted me, they let me into their homes, and what—I let the Ja-lal *ooh* and *aah* over their quaint animal ways? The newts couldn't possibly understand what I was planning to do, so they couldn't grant consent for me to share their private lives. And it's not like documenting stone lizard migration; the newts have troops. They have friends. I don't know if you can call them pyrsi. I don't know if you need to. They are no less important."

Ella looked away. "My editor had it all set up: private investors, a pen name, secret delivery. The Circles couldn't pin it on me. Even if they could, they wouldn't want to bring attention to it. I thought about taking out the details, just letting pyrsi know the newts are real. They're kind. They're not monsters. But who would read that? Who'd believe it? How would it help?"

From Ella's tight lips and pained expression, Dime had the sense that there was more. She waited.

"There is so much over the cliff, Dime. So much we don't understand."

Dime nodded slowly. "If *you* could go there, others could go there."

"It's not even difficult. Despite what you think in Lodon, pyrsi do it all the time. It's only going to take the wrong one. What if the Ja-lal understood the richness of the forest? What would happen to the newts then? To—" She drew a sharp breath.

"After all that, I picked the wrong side, didn't I? I kept their secrets from the prying eyes of the Ja-lal and then the Fo-ror ran them right out of the forest. We saw signs of it then, but we didn't think it would go so far. It did.

"The Beds, the place you stayed, is a shadow of a newt village. They live now, cold, hungry, and in exile on beaches that don't support them. And I haven't done a *violent* thing about it."

Ella stared at the horizon as the wind raced by. Dime tried to put together the pieces of Ella's tale while wondering how to raise the point that she hadn't mentioned Suzanne at all. Surely Suzanne didn't also live with newts.

After a bit, Ella continued. "When I refused to turn the piece in, after all the resources and latitude they'd given me to do it, my career was over. I told them I'd pay them back, but they didn't care. They got wordy with me and I got wordy back."

Dime thought about pyrsi actually crossing the Great Cliff. Interacting with the newts. With the Fo-ror. While she couldn't grasp the consequences of it, it was no longer a hard line in her mind. With a shock, she realized her world no longer ended at that cliff. And she would never see it that way again. She tried to imagine Lodon's reaction to Ella's story. Whether that line would blur for others, as well.

"You did a good thing," she offered, speaking slowly as she thought through it. "I mean, about the newts. Whatever the Fo-ror did to them, we might have made it worse."

"Perhaps," Ella said, tearing apart a longfruit. "It could also have been better."

The last few turns had given Dime many of these same thoughts. Doubt. Regret. She had survived it by knowing she needed to move forward. And Ella would too. "We should have talked more about the Heartland. But not the way your editor wanted." Dime exhaled. "Ella, we never know the consequences of our choices. We can only do what seems best at the time. And then look forward."

"That's what Suzanne said," Ella murmured. "Oh. That's what you asked. So, long story short, the newts were still in the forest then, though they'd been pushed out of their original home, 'Home Sha' in their language. It's by a lake," she explained, "so to them it was their own version of Sha just for them. And Suzanne was in the forest a lot, journeying far outside of the villages. She liked to explore, you could say. Always finding new plants, new spicebeds—"

Ella's speech sped up and she held her gaze away. "I ran into her in the forest, neither of us ran away, and . . . soon we were meeting there, whenever she could. But I wasn't going to live with the newts forever, so I returned to Lodon, as I've mentioned. Returned, ruined my career, and left. Built my own private tower with my savings, out on the edge of the old woods."

She waved in the direction they'd been traveling. "Harm your towers, Lodon." Ella struggled for her next words and Dime pretended not to notice the fe'pyr's water flask shaking in her hand. "It was too empty without her. I went back."

"Suzanne was there, in the Heartland, waiting for me." Ella breathed in. "She told her family about me, that I was Ja-lal. They were nice to me, at first. Oddly accepting. I could barely contain my excitement, that first biscuit together—well, they don't use the term. But there I was, with a whole family of Fo-ror, sharing food, and laughing. Then it started.

"They reminded Suzanne in whispers that I was uncivilized. An animal. They reminded her that we use currency for greed. That we cut the trees and mine the rocks. They hugged her and explained that life was difficult and sometimes confusing. They wouldn't stop. Meanwhile, they smiled at me and welcomed me to the family pots." Ella waved. "It's a food thing," she murmured. Then, changing tone, "I thought things were going well!"

She set the flask down against a clump of grass.

"When Suzanne left, she left with a temper." Ella kicked her heel against a loose rock. "She loved that forest. She loved it. More than anything. But she wouldn't go back. Not after the way they treated me."

It sounded to Dime that Suzanne did not love the forest more than anything, but it wasn't the point and so she held her tongue. Without warning, Ella stood up, gathered and wiped her dishes, grabbed the large sack, threw it over her shoulder, and grunted. "Not safe here; better to get home."

Dime didn't argue, but leaned against her walking stick and moved as best she could down the hill, away from her own.

"This is it," Ella said, as they approached the edge of a small ridge.

Dime had long been admiring the lines of spiky trees in the distance. She'd never been this far wesside; no assignments ever sent agents near the woods; it was said that the land was unpopulated, too close to the dark woods for safety. *Maybe I can make excuses for one more thing I haven't done on account of the Circles!*

Peering below, Dime was struck by awe at the unusual structure. Hidden from view by the steep crag, you'd almost need to know where the lone tower was to find it.

Unlike the towers of Lodon, painted with decorations of leaves and berries and branches, which now Dime understood were ironically native to the Undergrowth, Ella's tower was natural. No paint, no trim, no adornments—natural, leafy vines wound around the tower. Some panels were covered, some cross-hatched, and others almost bare.

She breathed in deeply, strong scents of pine and sap filling her nose. Birds chirped and screeched in the background.

Ella walked down an easy set of stone steps that had a solid rail to the side. Dime, relieved that she didn't have to drop down a rope or some other contraption, followed behind, her walking stick clacking against each stone step.

Pulling a chain from inside her tunic, Ella removed an old-looking, elaborate key and turned it in the door. Once they were both inside, Ella locked the door again and tucked the key, like a pendant, back into her clothing. By instinct, Dime felt uncomfortable at the implications of using a key for a home, but she had never lived out here, alone.

As if Dime weren't there, Ella rushed up the circular staircase to the second level. Without any etiquette to go by, Dime decided to follow. "Friend!" Ella called, rushing to the windowsill.

Across an expansive, old wood sill lay a dense, spreading cover of green. Plump little needles protruded in all directions. As Ella caressed them, they bent and popped back into place as if responding to her touch. "Friend," she murmured, tapping a finger into the soil. "I'll get you more water right away. And your sprinkle! Please, forgive me for being away."

Dime wasn't sure whether she should approach the plant. Instead, she offered it a greeting. "Friend, hello. I am Fe'Dime." Dime wasn't quite sure about talking to a plant, but as much as she owed Ella for the timely rescue, she wasn't going to disrespect her only mate.

Friend didn't answer, and so Dime continued to glance around the space. The round room was lined with framed sketches—of trees, shrubs, and structures that Dime were sure came from the Undergrowth. No, what did the Fo-ror call it—the Heartland. Perhaps she should start thinking of it that way. The Heartland. And the Fo-ror. *It is a new world,* Dime sighed. *No, this was always the world.*

Ella showed Dime where the food cellar opened, where the washroom tunnel was, and a bed where she could rest. Turning to her kitchen, Ella lit the stove and began pulling apart a hunk of dried crumble. "We've had enough fruit," she said. "Figured a hearty stew would do."

Dime felt at home as she and Ella sat down to a warm stew, smelling of rich broth and complex spices. "Delicious," Dime sighed.

"So I don't want to keep mentioning her; it sounds like I have an issue or something, but cooking was Suzanne's specialty. She knew every plant and herb: which had good flavor, which preserved well, which could be made into doughs, curds, pulps, and deins. This dein, it's a barley and mushroom base. Makes in big batches and keeps a whole season. You can roll it into balls, fry it, use it in stews—it's my favorite."

Ella stared at her full spoon. Dime paused her own eating, not wanting to seem rude.

"For her, it was a rebellion," Ella said, her speech accelerating. "Her family received standard foods, per their class, yet Suzanne took great delight in making her family a daily feast fit for the High Seat, elevated by a range of spices.

"One night, someone's stomach ailment was eased by a salad she made, and so she began exploring medicinal uses, including the rarer plants outforest. Before long, she was making teas and medicines for anyone who would accept them from her." Ella dropped her spoon into the bowl. "She was a washer, per their society. Was supposed to stick to that." Ella's expression was fond, though sad.

"She was lonely here. She'd never say it, but who wouldn't know. I offered to leave with her; I'd go anywhere. But, she was attached to this place too by then, to our little haunted woods. The Heartland, it was not. But it was someplace."

Dime finished her soup and helped Ella rinse out the dishes. Ella turned with a pained expression. "We have more to discuss."

A knot turned in Dime's stomach. She had delivered difficult news before and could sense that Ella was gathering the courage to push the words out. She couldn't imagine what a stranger would have to tell her that could be so bad. That would be more shocking than a Fo-ror as spouse. Or the resurgence of Sol's Pillars. And she'd said she had no news about Dime's family, so it wasn't that.

"Look," Dime offered, hoping to ease the tension, "if there's a prophecy about a career-quitting fe'pyr who falls off a cliff, and all I have to do is climb the high mountain and convene with the fairy queen, you might as well tell me now. I'm the chosen one, right? That's where this is going?"

"You read too much." Ella managed a nervous grin.

No such thing. "I'm ready for it. There's something. So, don't worry; I can handle it. At this point, I can handle anything." Dime laughed.

Ella shook her head, wandered to the cabinet, and poured herself a thick brown liquid. She shot it down, wincing.

"I'm making you a new jacket."

This was the secret? Dime looked down at her jacket. The only clothing she still wore from her run through the city, the plains, the forest, the beaches, the grasslands, and back through the plains, it was indeed in tatters. An update would be welcome, as long as it had enough pockets. Pockets were handy. "Thank you. You've already done so much for me, though."

Ella cleared her throat. "May I see your back? I don't know how else to ask. It's . . . related to your injuries." Her eyes shifted to the side.

Dime had always been self-conscious about her back, and even more so since the newts had found it so novel. Pyrsi were quick to compliment her interesting tattoo, not knowing it was hiding her scars. Scars she didn't understand but must have been related to some mishandling as a ba'pyr. Even if it hadn't been her father, and she didn't think it had, she'd not wanted to upset him by asking about it.

The request was uncomfortable, but Ella's expression was somber. Turning around, Dime removed her jacket and untied the loose tunic Ella had brought her. Now, only the fabric band holding her breasts snug remained. "That's enough," Ella said. "I'm not trying to get fresh here. Now, please, just a moment."

Ella walked around to her back. Dime could not see her and waited, agitation growing, during a pronounced silence.

"May I touch you?"

"Sure," Dime answered. At this point, she was going with it.

Ella ran her thin fingers over Dime's back and under her straps, pausing at her scars. "You have a father," she whispered. "From birth?"

"Almost from birth. My father found me, alone in one of the upper corridors of the Circles' complex. He worked for the Maintenance Circle. Stone repair, mostly. He checked with the local medical enclave and with the clerk, and there was no record. Aromantic, single, and halfway through his Bakh, he . . . well, it's like he saw me as a gift from Sol. My father is a strong believer in Sol."

"And your children—forgive my rude question, but are they biological?"

"No." Dime didn't like involving her children in whatever was happening and didn't know why their biology would be relevant. "The medical enclave knew my history and offered them to us. To Dayn and me. He's my spouse."

Ella reached for Dime's shirt and drew it back into place over her shoulders. Instinctively Dime closed the front wrap. She turned to look at Ella, whose face was drawn.

"You are a Fo-ror."

Dime stared back. *I can't be a Fo-ror, they have—* She gasped.

"I don't know, Dime. If it was done on purpose, it is an act of the Violence as I have never seen or imagined. And it does look to be on purpose, with the precision of a skilled surgeon. The newts knew this right away, just from the sense of you, I suppose. I wasn't sure I believed them. Your slight sight in the dark, your slowness in healing, your instinct to relax by night—these are all Fo-ror traits. Your spouse . . . if he is Ja-lal, then you could not conceive."

"Can I have a shot of that now?" was all Dime could muster.

Ella poured her one and brought it over. Dime threw it back, wincing much harder than Ella had. "Oh, it's terrible."

"I know. Suzanne insisted I take it once a turn. It might still be a prank, but she died before I remembered to ask her."

Their eyes met. "I'm really a . . . *fairy*?" Dime didn't believe her own words.

"I believe so."

"What the kill does that mean?"

Ella opened her hands. "I have no idea. I truly do not. But your quitting the Circles . . . that timing is not coincidence. I've thought about that a lot. We need to know who came for you, which faction. Can you describe anything about them?"

Dime thought. She only really saw the one whose robe was pulled off by Dayn's claw. She could see xyr face; she'd never forget it, but not in any way she could describe.

"Xe had a long face, possibly masculine. No tattoos, though I suppose that's normal. If their skin is like ours, xe was older than me. With long hair, braided like rope—it was dark, like almost black. Once xyr cloak was torn off, I could see xe wore a dark gown, with natural shoulders, and a small crystal pin." Dime searched her memories. "The others had lighter hair, but I only saw them from a distance. I'm sorry; that's all I remember."

"A crystal pin! Was it shaped like this?" Ella scrambled to find a scrap of paper and drew a circle, surrounded by a wavy border.

That did look right. "Yes, I think so."

Ella sat down again. "Your necklace, you know it's an uncut diamond?"

"Yes," Dime said, reaching to clasp it in her hand.

"Diamonds are sacred to the Fo-ror. They amplify valence, help focus its energy. And so the crystals are protected, or hoarded depending on your view. Very few have access to the caves, and fewer are able to carry stones with them. That pendant you wear, it is precious to the Fo-ror. And the pin you describe, it is the insignia of someone acting on behalf of the Seats."

"The Seats? I presume that's like our Light's Circle?"

"Yes, and also no. Yes in equivalence, but their governance is different. The Circles, as corrupt as they are—don't look at me that way—at least have a pretense of balance. The Light chooses the members of the Light's Circle, yet only continues to serve with the approval of the Light's Circle. Circle members may retire, and if they work and persevere hard enough, they may come from the lower class. Like you."

Dime's involuntary reaction almost knocked the shot glass to one side. She caught it with the other hand, releasing the diamond, which fell back onto her chest.

"The Seats also choose their own, but they are much more bound by tradition and class. The Seats are chosen for life, and seniority alone determines rank. Dime, I'd thought perhaps some radical group or someone seeking a reward had learned something about you or your pendant and sought to take you to the Heartland. But the Seats. Sha's blessings, Dime."

Unfounded conspiracies presented as facts were one of Dime's sticking points. *No faster way to foster division and ill will.* "You can't know it was their rulers just because of a pin. Anyone could wear a pin."

"True," Ella said with a nod. "Though stealing diamonds to impyrsinate a High Guard would earn you a long haul in the dead caves. I've never heard of it."

"And you've heard of Fo-ror flying through Lodon?"

"No. Now that you mention it."

"They said I was getting a rest." Dime was still unsettled by what that meant.

Ella winced. "No. *Arrest.* Fo-ror justice. When a pyr commits a crime, xe is taken against xyr will and locked away for a period in a prison, to rethink and rework xyr ways."

"*Against xyr will?* How is that permitted?"

Ella half-snorted, half-laughed. "Right, and marking xem for life to warn others is? Altering xem and effectively driving them from the city, from xyr career? From xyr family? Driving xem to move to an outer ring or outlaw village, where xe is more likely to be accepted? Just to be treated as a pyr?"

Hemsa weren't viewed as forced, but they weren't optional either. It was just a way of life. The way of things. *Ugh, the fallacies in that logic.* Dime felt tired. She released her grip on the shot glass and leaned back.

Ella tapped the table. "Look, I know there have to be rules. But maybe not so many? And maybe more nuanced ways to enforce them? Ways that don't impact some pyrsi more than others? Ways that give a pyr a chance? Nope. No one wants to talk about any of it. Not and risk disrupting the peace. Risking the Violence. Oh, I wouldn't want to get on your little Circles' list, would I?

"But—" she flung up a hand. "the Violence is gone! Hooray! Does anyone believe that? Doesn't matter. Always silence."

Not silence. But she wasn't going to argue; her own advocacy against hemsa had been widely dismissed and Dime didn't like wallowing in some weird self-pity about it. And now, with this growing realization that hemsa were just some sanitized version of the Violence anyway, she was doubting even her own voice.

She clearly hadn't been as radical as she'd thought.

Ella shifted back in her chair. "Sorry, it's just— Here's something I've learned: *Hiding* the Violence doesn't reduce it. Wherever this takes you, remember to think about that."

The idea of her own scars fresh on her mind, Dime resolved that she would.

Trying to focus, she replayed the fairies' intrusion in her mind, first at her home and then in the street. She wished now that she'd noted the details at the time, rather than trying to construct them now. But she hadn't been prepared; it had happened so quickly. And been so *strange.*

Once they were uncloaked, she'd been mostly distracted by their wings and hair, but she'd noticed the pin because it caught her eye over the plain robes. That fairy hadn't spoken, just the other one. *Meet at Chambers.*

Dime spoke slowly, still trying to think if there was anything else. "Xe mentioned returning to 'Chambers,' I think. When they decided to separate. The pin was as you described. I don't know what else there is."

Ella grimaced. "Chambers is where they meet. It all fits. Of course, that doesn't make it true. Yet . . . I don't see them staging a comment like that. No reason they'd think you'd understand it."

As Ella stood and walked toward the window, Dime forced herself to consider what Ella had said. She didn't think of herself as a fairy; she didn't think that she could. Yet, there was something true of it in her gut. If so, had she been betrayed by her own kind? Left to die? And now, turns later, Sol's Pillars operated in the open in Lodon. Dime had done nothing. Nothing at all.

Dime noticed that Ella was watching her.

"I feel it too," Ella said. "Everything's changed and I don't know why. I only know one thing: you are in the middle of all of it, Diamond of the Ja-lal." There was no sarcasm in Ella's tone, yet the words stung. She *was* a Ja-lal. Could that be taken away so easily?

Dime tried again to piece together everything she had learned, everything she was learning. She had left one government just to be declared, what had they called it, under arrest by the other. And what she still didn't have was *information*. Dime's hand closed around her pendant, and its tiny chain harness pressed into her skin.

"Ella?"

"Yes."

"Could you make some brew? I could use some. Also, where are these Seats located?"

"In Pito, their largest city. It rests near the main entrance to the caves. The current High Seat is Ma'Ferala, a high Dorh. Though," she added with a grimace, "only a cycle older than me. So you know, young and spry. Fit for the ages."

"Is it safe there? With the Fo-ror?"

"Sure, as safe as Lodon." Ella shrugged.

"Well then, I'm going to Pito."

"What!" Ella exclaimed. "We just got you away from them. You've lost your compass!"

Dime glanced at her wrist, glad to see the band in place. "You just said it was as safe as Lodon. If I can deal with one government, I can deal with another. They're all the same, aren't they? Pyrsi who love power. Sure, some have better motivations than others, but in the end, it's power they seek. The power to control or the power to assist. Either way, I'm used to it.

"I need to figure out what's going *on*. Do you think anyone in Lodon has those answers?"

A take or two passed as they sat across the table from each other, avoiding each other's direct gaze. Ella rose and began to heat the water for brew. She soaked and pressed the beans, ran the brew through the filter, and poured it into two large mugs. All the time, Dime watched the birds flying past the window. She watched Friend sitting quietly on its ledge. She smelled the richness of the fine quality beans that Ella possessed, as fine as the tastes in food that Suzanne had taught her.

It wasn't until the rich brew was mostly gone that Ella let out a deep sigh. "Fairies," she said. "I have one request. You'll need your strength. Your ankle is almost stable. Your wound is almost closed. You'll want to shave; unless you want to go in there with that stubbly cap—I wouldn't recommend it. I'll sew you clothes that fit, and a new jacket. Boots built for mud. Stay here a couple more turns. I'll check on your family. We'll get them a message. Please."

Dime had to admit that sounded reasonable.

"Ella, I'm so grateful for all you've done for me. I'll take you up on your two turns. And then I'm going to find this High Seat myself and . . . sit him in his seat . . . and ask him why he wants me." Dime grinned, a feeling of control returning for the first time in turns. "Besides, he might want me less this time, when I'm ready for him."

"Sha's Blessings, fairies *are* stubborn," Ella murmured.

"Oh, I'm certain they all aren't," Dime mused. "But, sure, this one is."

For the first time since they'd met, Ella smiled. Dime warmed with joy at seeing the light break across the fe'pyr's weary face. A spark lit within Dime's spirit.

Had she given up? *No*, she decided. *I've only just begun.*

END OF PART 01

ABOUT THE AUTHOR

E.D.E. Bell was born in the year of the fire dragon during a Cleveland blizzard. With an MSE in Electrical Engineering from the University of Michigan, three wonderful children, and nearly two decades in Northern Virginia and Southwest Ohio developing technical intelligence strategy, she now applies her magic to the creation of genre-bending fantasy fiction in Ferndale, Michigan, where she is proud to be part of the Detroit arts community. A passionate vegan and enthusiastic denier of gender rules, she feels strongly about issues related to human equality and animal compassion. She revels in garlic. She loves cats and trees. You can follow her adventures at edebell.com.

Follow Dime's story in . . .

Part 02: Capture

edebell.com/diamondsong